Look what people are saying about Julie Elizabeth Leto...

"Ms. Leto's signature steam comes through loud and clear."
—*Fallen Angel Reviews* on *Line of Fire*

"Julie Elizabeth Leto does it again with another great read! Danger, mystery, suspense, romance and well, lots of hot sex."
—*The Best Reviews* on *Brazen & Burning*

"Sizzling chemistry and loads of sexual tension make this Leto tale a scorcher."
—*Romantic Times BOOKreviews* on "Chasing Charlie"

"This book not only singed my fingers but it also burned my eyes! Another hot, one-sitting read from Julie Elizabeth Leto!"
—*The Best Reviews* on *Double the Pleasure*

"A streak of sensuousness not often seen in traditional series romance. Bravo!"
—*A Romance Review* on *Up To No Good*

"Graced with a sassy heroine and a hero with just the right amount of vulnerability, this story boasts witty dialogue, passionate encounters and a wonderful whirlwind romance."
—*Romantic Times BOOKreviews* on "My Lips Are Sealed"

Blaze™

Dear Reader,

Welcome back to the BAD GIRLS CLUB!

Bad Girls. Harlequin Blaze. I can't imagine a better combination. Wait. Yes, I can. Make it a miniseries that reunites the authors who launched the series back in Harlequin Temptation—Tori Carrington, Leslie Kelly and me. Yeah, that rocks.

What was also amazing about writing the series in Blaze was getting permission to really push the book and the characters to the limit. The only rule in the bad girls club is to break all the rules. So in this story, I'm going to bring you deep into a paranormal world. My heroine, Lilith St. Lyon, is a real witch. And by that I mean a *real* witch. She's more Serena than Samantha Stevens, admittedly... but that's what makes her so much fun.

If you enjoy Lilith's story, please keep an eye out for her sister Regina's story next month in the Harlequin anthology *Witchy Business!* For excerpts and more information, visit me at www.julieleto.com or at my blog with my plotting partners, www.plotmonkeys.com.

Happy reading!

Julie

JULIE ELIZABETH LETO
Stripped

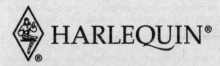

TORONTO • NEW YORK • LONDON
AMSTERDAM • PARIS • SYDNEY • HAMBURG
STOCKHOLM • ATHENS • TOKYO • MILAN • MADRID
PRAGUE • WARSAW • BUDAPEST • AUCKLAND

ISBN-13: 978-0-373-79345-7
ISBN-10:   0-373-79345-6

STRIPPED

ABOUT THE AUTHOR

With twenty-six novels under her belt, *New York Times* and *USA TODAY* bestselling author Julie Elizabeth Leto has established a reputation for writing ultra-sexy, edgy stories. Julie writes primarily for the Harlequin Blaze line and was part of the series launch in 2001, as well as the fifth anniversary in 2006. A 2005 RITA® Award nominee, Julie lives in her hometown of Tampa with her husband, daughter and a very spoiled dachshund. For more information, check out Julie's Web site at www.julieleto.com.

Books by Julie Elizabeth Leto

Special thanks to Elissa Wilds, for sharing
her knowledge and her love of her craft so that
I could ground my fictional characters in
the very real community.

Shout outs to Brenda Chin, Tori Carrington
and Leslie Kelly, for once again bringing the
Bad Girls Club back to life...with a vengeance.
Drinks are on me.

And as always, to the Plotmonkeys.

Prologue

"YOU CAN'T BE SERIOUS."

Lilith St. Lyon slapped the newest muscle-car magazine on her coffee table and slammed to her feet. She really hated when her sister barged in without as much as a call. Or a simple knock. Hell, even a whisper along the lines of *Excuse me, sis, but I'm about to shimmer into your apartment, so don't get freaked* would suffice.

Sometimes Lilith hated being a witch.

Especially when Regina showed up all regal in her deep-purple robes, flaunting how she could bypass Lilith's psychic powers and appear without warning. One advantage of Lilith's talent was that, for the most part, no one could sneak up on her. No one except the most powerful witch in the realm— her big sis. Yet here she was, startled, pissed and staring daggers at Regina, gorgeous as always with her flowing dark hair and penetrating lilac eyes, and the gray-haired, pinched-faced members of the Witches Council who flanked Regina on either side.

"Lilith St. Lyon, you are charged—" Regina started, but Lilith cut her off by kicking over the coffee table. Her boots shattered the glass and scattered her magazines to the floor in a glossy, jagged heap.

The councillors jumped back, their arms instantly stiff in defensive postures Lilith could bypass with another swift kick. Regina remained still.

So in control. So royal. So damned perfect Lilith wanted to puke. Or scream.

"Don't do this, Reg," Lilith ordered.

Lilith tried to ignore the pained look on her sister's face. Regina hadn't asked for this gig, but she sure took the whole power trip seriously. Had since day one. Not that she'd had any choice in the matter.

"Lilith, you've given the Council no other recourse."

"You're the freaking Guardian," Lilith shouted, sweeping her hand toward Regina's amulet, the silver-dollar-size alexandrite that dangled from a platinum chain and glowed red and blue and green just between her breasts. "You can tell the Council where to shove their asinine rules. Or, better yet, shimmer *all* their fogy asses over here and I'll tell them myself. You can't take my powers."

As a powerful psychic, Lilith knew that was exactly what her sister had come here to do. Though, honestly, she didn't need clairvoyance to figure it out. Lilith had known the rules before she'd broken them. No utilizing powers for personal gain. First her mother and then her aunt Marion had tried for years to drill the concept into her brain. But Lilith couldn't understand why, if she had to live with all the crap that accompanied being a living, breathing witch of the higher realm, she couldn't also have a few of the finer things in life to make the sacrifices worthwhile.

"The Council does not fear you," Regina said, her mouth twitching.

She was lying. Oh, Regina herself wasn't afraid of Lilith.

As Guardian, Regina had no reason to fear anyone except the occasional witch hunter or warlock or demon. She and Lilith had broken in their wands sparring together, even after Regina's powers had grown so that she no longer needed carved teak to focus her magic. Lilith had long ago accepted that she'd never wield the type of magic Regina could, even after her psychic powers had come into their own. And that was fine by her. She'd seen her sister's future. Picnics were not on the schedule.

"The Council has lived apart from mundanes too long," Lilith countered. "They don't remember what life in the normal world is like. We're sisters, Reg. The bond we share runs deeper than rules and regulations, even those carved into stone tablets shortly after the dawn of humanity."

Regina's expression softened, but the Council was another story. The twin towers of old-world thought that stood one to each side of her sister swirled with auras white with fear and admonition. Everyone in the witching world feared Lilith, reviled her even—had her whole life—though Lilith could never quite understand why. Sure, she had a habit of losing her temper and hurling epithets with more precision than a major league pitcher. Her psychic prophecies had sometimes caused distress here and there. But in the long run she was just a sassy pain in the ass. Her powers were nothing compared to her sister's. It's not as though she could blow anybody up.

"I need my powers, Reg," Lilith whispered.

"You no longer deserve them," Regina countered, her gaze glittering purple like the stone of rank she wore around her neck.

"Do you hear how you sound like a complete hypocrite?"

Regina sucked in a breath. For a split second Lilith felt guilty. Then she got over it.

Four years older, Regina had been barely a teenager when she'd been tapped as Guardian following their mother's brutal murder at the hands of a warlock. But unlike most witches attacked by the thieving race of witch killers, their mother had transferred her powers to her older daughter before she died. From that moment, Regina possessed a wide range of powers that included being able to shimmer from one place to another and the ability to form and hurl energy bursts that could blast a demon or warlock to kingdom come—an act Regina had executed only seconds after their mother had taken her last breath.

Baptism by fire, literally. There might not have been as many demons and warlocks in the world as a certain popular television show about witches might lead one to believe, but when one popped up, the burst had come in damn handy. And for this everyone loved Regina.

All Lilith could do was read minds and predict the future. And even then, sometimes her predictions came too late.

As it had for her mother.

She swallowed the lump in her throat and stood firm.

"What about all the good I do with my powers?" Lilith argued. "My work with the cops?"

Regina arched a brow. "You abruptly stopped working with the police three months ago."

Lilith had the insatiable need to stick her tongue out. "I can't help it if they don't call me anymore."

A smile twitched Regina's generous lips—a family trait. St. Lyon women never needed collagen.

"Can't you?" she asked knowingly. "And, besides, can you honestly tell us that you have gained nothing personally from your association with the police?"

Not without lying.

Lilith had gained plenty—first and foremost, major bedroom action with chief of detectives, Mac Mancusi. But that was over. Had been since he'd figured out that she was a real psychic and not simply an ultra-intuitive woman, as he'd rationalized. Oh, and that she'd been using her powers to manipulate him into falling head over heels in love with her. Yeah, that had pretty much sealed him kicking her ass to the curb.

"My benefits were short-lived and not without repercussions," Lilith said, jabbing her hand through her spiky short hair. "I'm on my own again. Just me and all the bad guys I help the cops catch whenever they come to me. I could clean up Chicago once and for all."

"And disrupt the balance of good and evil?" Regina asked, her voice hitching higher than her normal sultry tone. "Jeez, Lilith, are there no rules you won't break?"

Lilith stamped her foot, crunching down on a large, serrated glass triangle. "The only rules I won't break are the ones I make for myself."

"Like?"

Lilith scowled. She wasn't a big rule maker. She definitely ascribed to a live-and-let-live philosophy. "I do no harm, Regina."

"What do you call the aftermath experienced by your clients once you've bilked them for a peek at their futures?"

"It's not *bilking* if what I tell them is true," she countered. "If they can't handle the truth, that's their problem."

The two elders on either side of Regina whispered simultaneously in her sister's ear.

Once again, her smart mouth wasn't helping. Nothing would. No amount of pouting or manipulating was going to get her out of this one. She did a quick probe of their minds. They wanted her powers. The future of order in the witching world depended on Lilith's punishment. Blah, blah, blah.

Regina nodded to the elders, then with a swish of her hand, shimmered them out of the room.

Lilith took a hopeful step forward.

"What just happened?"

"I don't need them to witness what must be done."

Betrayal cut a slash through her heart. "Reggie, you can't."

Her sister's eyes glossed with emotion. "You've given me no choice, Lilith. Please take the punishment the Council has chosen. Use this time as a mundane to prove to them you are capable of selfless good, and maybe you can earn your powers back."

Instinctively Lilith squared her shoulders and lifted her chin. "The Council can kiss my ass."

Regina quirked a quick half grin before she placed her hands gently on Lilith—one hand on her forehead and the other on her heart.

She made short work of the incantation, a spell as old as time itself. Lilith planted her feet solidly on the ground, refusing to yield as her psychic energy was sucked out of her. She loved her sister, but if she'd had the strength at that moment, she would have coldcocked her as soon as the spell was complete.

Instead she drifted to the floor, unconscious and unaware of how deeply her life had just been irrevocably changed.

1

"YOU HAVE TO CALL HER."

Mac Mancusi stood, eyes focused on his perp on the other side of the one-way mirror. The jackass was forcing his hand. With teeth grinding until his jaw ached, Mac cursed. There had to be another way to save this case before it was flushed down the crapper, his career along with it.

"I don't *have* to do anything, Fernandez. Last time I checked, I was still the chief of detectives in this department. Or did your sorry ass somehow get promoted by the new mayor when I was wiping his footprints off my back?"

Through the reflection in the glass, Mac watched Lt. Rick Fernandez run his hand through his thick hair.

"Boss, I'm just saying… We all know the mayor's been riding you since the election. His smarmy staff boys have been sniffing around the precinct all week, hunting for some damning shit to leak to the press. If this drug bust doesn't happen, you can kiss your job goodbye."

Mac forced his words through his tight lips. "I know the stakes."

"Then why are you waiting around? Call the *bruja!*"

Sounded so easy. Call the witch who'd ripped his heart out, filleted it, then served it on an Italian roll with onions, peppers and a side of you're-a-fool. Yeah, no problem. Wasn't as if he had any pride or anything as inconvenient as self-respect to stand in his way.

"Know what, Fernandez? I remember a time when this department could beat a confession out of a perp without having to call some voodoo princess to do our dirty work."

Fernandez shoved his hands in his pockets. "Listen, boss, you want to beat the crap out of Pogo Goins and hope he gives up the location of three hundred kilos of cocaine, I'll back you up. But you know that shit won't fly anymore. We need the location of the drugs and we need it two hours ago. I don't know what happened between you and Lilith, but it can't be as bad as what's going to happen if we don't find that blow before it hits the streets. Word is the shit ain't pure. We're going to have ODs, turf wars, retaliations. Chaos. Goins hasn't asked for a lawyer yet. He still thinks we're talking to him about his stolen car. We don't have much time before his brain clears enough to know we're trying to flip him for the information. He'll call his mouthpiece for sure."

And then the interview would be over. Mac and the detectives in his department didn't have anything to hold Pogo Goins, just a tip that the low-level hood had been the go-between in a huge shipment of cocaine. When Goins's car went missing and he actually reported it to the cops, the Chicago PD had gotten the break they'd been waiting for—a chance to put a real dent in the drug trade, maybe even take down the masterminds behind the renewed influx of high-priced, low-quality coke. If the rumors were true and the drugs weren't pure, the stakes went through the roof.

Time was running out. He needed Lilith.

"Go grab a pack of cigarettes for our guest," Mac said,

gritting out the words between his tightened teeth, "while I make a call."

Rick grinned, gave a quick nod, then headed out, closing the door behind him.

Mac pulled out his cell phone and hit the speed-dial button he'd yet to delete. When Lilith didn't instantly answer, his stomach hardened. She used to pick up on the first ring— sometimes before. She claimed to always know when he was calling. He figured she had caller ID and a less-than-busy work schedule predicting future love matches for idiots with too much disposable income.

But today she ignored his call.

Maybe she didn't want to talk to him.

He couldn't blame her.

When he'd figured out exactly how she'd become his perfect lover, how she'd always known exactly when he wanted to talk and when chatter was the last thing on his mind, he'd never been so angry, so confused, so completely infuriated. He'd heard crime victims say they'd felt violated after a rape or robbery, and while he'd understood them on an intellectual level, he'd never truly accepted the full meaning until he'd learned what Lilith really was.

Not a clever con woman.

Not a supersmart people watcher.

Not even a deeply intuitive woman.

Nope, she was a psychic.

A real one.

The kind only fools believed in. The kind only bigger fools fell in love with.

He buried his cell phone in his pocket and charged out of the observation room and into his office. He buzzed the switchboard and asked them to dial Lilith's number from a secured line.

After four rings, she finally picked up.

"Lilith St. Lyon."

"Hey," he said.

Pause. Long pause. The kind of pause that made his teeth hurt.

"Lilith? It's Mac."

"And I thought my day couldn't get any worse."

"I'm thrilled to hear your voice, too," he couldn't help snapping.

She hung up.

Damn.

On a string of bluer curses, he had the switchboard dial again.

This time she waited six rings to pick up.

"What do you want, Mancusi?"

He should have expected her cold response, but *he* was supposed to be pissed off at *her*. Not the other way around.

He cleared his throat. "We've got a case."

"How nice for you."

"We need your…input."

"Too bad. I'm out of business."

Mac shoved a few files off to the side of his desk and leaned his hip against the hard surface. She could be so damn stubborn.

"Look, Lilith, clearly you're still pissed at me."

"Ooh, do you suddenly possess the evil clairvoyance? Aren't you afraid of yourself?"

"I wasn't afraid of you," he insisted, affronted.

She sighed, her tone lilting with disbelief. "I'm hanging up now," she said. "Not that I need to tell you that. You already knew, right?"

"Hey, those cracks should be coming from me, not you," he barked.

"Maybe I've developed a new skill—channeling! Either way, I don't want to talk to you any more than you want to talk to me."

"Then talk to Fernandez," Mac offered, thinking quickly. His lead detective viewed Lilith with a mixture of fear and respect, topped off with a heavy dose of good old-fashioned lust. Every guy in the department had the hots for the woman, and he couldn't blame them. He'd bullied every single one of them out of his way on the path to her bed. Slim, sleek and brunette, Lilith strutted to a soundtrack of "Black Magic Woman." But despite Mac's territorial warnings to the men he supervised, Lilith and Fernandez had struck up a weird friendship. Mac wasn't beyond exploiting the relationship for his own benefit. He'd learned some lessons from her very, very well.

"Rick's in on this?"

"The whole department is. This case isn't a joke. We're talking large quantities of drugs about to hit the streets unless we can pry the location of the stash out of Pogo Goins."

"Goins? He's a moron," Lilith snapped. "Why would he have such high-level information?"

"That's what I want to know."

Silence. Mac replayed the conversation in his mind while he waited. He definitely had her interest. That much he knew without any extrasensory perception.

"I'll be there in a half hour," she said, her voice resigned.

"Fifteen minutes."

"Twenty if you're lucky. And I want my hot water ready, got it?"

She disconnected the call.

Mac placed the handset down gently on the cradle, his breathing surprisingly even, though a little deeper than usual. A smile teased the edge of his lips, but the moment he acknowledged the warmth of laughter in his chest, the emotion turned to ice. He couldn't afford to let his guard down. He'd called her. He'd heard her voice. Sparred with her. He couldn't allow the old feelings to resurface.

Except the anger.

Mac knew he had to drop this resentment, but it was hard to let go when Lilith's secret abilities had caught him so completely off guard. The revelation had wrecked what he thought might have been the relationship of a lifetime. They'd been só compatible. So in sync. But that had been an illusion. A con. She'd used her powers to become his perfect partner. She'd stripped away his free will. Made him fall in love.

Lord, how pathetic.

Except for the one supersize secret of her psychic ability, Lilith had been the quintessential what-you-see-is-what-you-get woman. And now that he thought about it, she hadn't really kept a secret at all. She'd said from the start that she was a genuine clairvoyant. He'd simply never believed her.

Sure, he'd used her in his investigations, having met her when the parents of a missing child had begged her to help find their daughter. He remembered their first encounter vividly. She'd been in the little girl's room. Alone. Lightly fingering a tiny porcelain tea set, her eyes glossy, her cheeks streaked. She didn't try to cover up her emotions when he barged in but instead threw them at him like weapons. She'd been raw and uninhibited and larger than life. He'd instantly realized that she wasn't some charlatan trying to raise false hopes in the hearts of desperate parents. She hadn't wanted to be there. She hadn't wanted to help. But she had, and the child who had disappeared without a clue, without a trace, had been recovered in less than twelve hours.

Mac tried to remember exactly how he'd rationalized her talents back then, but accepting that she possessed real extra-sensory power had never been an option. He'd simply attributed her talents to hypersensitivity in reading other people. The missing child's stepfather had, after all, been involved in the kid-napping. She'd realized quickly that he had been lying and had not only produced the child relatively unharmed, but had also helped Mac wrangle a confession that had held up in court.

After her initial performance, Mac had authorized her to work with the department, mostly with interrogations. She was more reliable than any polygraph and much nicer to look at than a department examiner. He'd established a comfortable sexual banter with her that inevitably exploded into a full-blown affair the night he'd lost a detective in the line and she'd shown up as if she'd known someone had ripped a hole in his gut.

From that night on he'd ignored all the other signs that pointed him toward facts he couldn't accept. How could one person know what another person was thinking? He'd made a conscious effort to never lie to her, since she was so adept at ferreting out the truth, but he'd never in a million years imagined that she could creep into his psyche and extract tiny facts and fantasies he'd never admit to out loud.

And now, with her on her way back into the precinct and his life, he wouldn't be able to hide anything from her.

Or from himself—and that rankled most of all.

"I'M SO GLAD I CAUGHT YOU!"

Lilith swung around, flattening her back against the just-locked door to her apartment. Her heart slammed against her chest, then tried to pound its way out. She hadn't heard anyone come up behind her. Hell, she hadn't *felt* anyone. Until she'd lost her powers, she hadn't realized how dependent she'd become on her magical abilities.

Which is the whole point of losing them, she could hear her sister say.

"Shut up," Lilith spat under her breath.

Josie Vargas's blond eyebrows shot up under her wispy bangs. "Excuse me?" Josie marched to a stop, her hand clutching the pentacle charm she wore around her neck.

"Wasn't cursing at you, Josie," Lilith said, rolling her eyes at her own stupidity, "just at myself. I've got to bolt. Can I catch up with you later?"

Josie's eyes widened. A practicing Wiccan, Josie wrote spells, worshipped the god and goddess and led rituals for her small coven. She brewed potions from time to time, but her main talent was in creating candles enhanced with essential oils.

She was an ordinary witch. A mundane. No active powers.

Like Lilith. Not before, but now.

Despite her lack of tangible powers, however, Josie always seemed to know when Lilith was up to something—particularly when she was marching straight into disaster.

"Where are you headed in such a hurry?" Josie asked, her tone omniscient.

"The police station."

"Mac's police station?"

"There are hundreds of police stations in the city. And yet I keep going back to the same one. Isn't that a sign of insanity or something?"

"Possibly, since Mac is hot and you're in love with him."

Lilith's jaw dropped open.

Josie tapped her under the chin with her finger. "Don't gape. It's unattractive."

"I'm. Not. In. Love. With. Mac."

Josie nodded condescendingly. "Then why are you going to the police station?"

Lilith growled as she stuffed her keys into her hip bag. In contrast to Josie's purse, which was roughly the size of Lake Michigan, Lilith's bag contained three items. Her keys, her favorite lip gloss and cash. She wondered how much longer she'd have any spending money now that she'd been stripped of her ability to do psychic readings. Too bad the cops didn't pay her one red cent. Other than all the herbal tea she could drink and a sense of accomplishment, she didn't get a damn thing from the department. Though without her powers she wasn't sure she'd be any use at all.

Still, she couldn't bring herself to tell Mac no. As much as she'd wanted to, as much as the logical part of her brain screamed at her to stay clear of her former lover, she couldn't deny him.

He needed her.

And she needed him. Or at least, his case. If the Council wanted to witness her good and selfless heart, they could watch her now. So she wasn't psychic at the moment. She'd find a way to help.

If nothing else, she could flaunt what she hoped Mac was seriously missing from his life—namely, her in his bed.

She'd chosen her outfit with extreme care. Tight jeans. See-through blouse. Skintight tank underneath. Killer spiked boots. Of course, she wouldn't *know* if her primping truly enticed him since her powers were gone. Though, how hard could it be for a woman to figure out if a man wanted her? Even ordinary women knew.

Ordinary.

Lilith blanched, then vowed to never, ever be ordinary.

"Did you need something, Josie?"

Discussion of Mac visibly flew out of Josie's brain. "I had a really odd dream last night."

Dream interpretation had never been Lilith's forte. She marched toward the elevator, trying to psych herself up for seeing Mac again. Smelling Mac again. Hopefully feeling Mac again, even if it was just a brush of hands or a shoulder bump.

"You know I can't help you with that."

Josie huffed. "Hello? Not everyone who hangs out with you *wants* something. I didn't come to you as a psychic. I came to you as a friend."

Lilith winced and turned slowly.

"Sorry. You know I suck at the whole interpersonal-relationship thing. I'm too self-absorbed."

Josie took a step back. "You say that as if you think it's a bad thing."

"It is according to the majority of people in my life."

Josie joined her friend across the hall and pushed the down button. "Well, yeah, but I've never heard you say so. Since when did you get self-awareness?"

"I've had a life-changing experience," she muttered.

"Something bad?"

Nothing she could talk about. Well, she could tell Josie. There wasn't actually a witch law that forbade her from revealing herself to a mundane. But centuries of history proved it wasn't a good idea. Regular people tended not to believe in the paranormal. Dumping such a wild story on her pal would mean she'd risk losing the one and only person beyond her sister that she considered a close friend. Most Wiccans who, like Josie, studied the craft and worshipped the deities never realized that there was a level of witches that existed between the mundane and the divine. Witches with powers that, without utmost secrecy, could be exposed. Some witches possessed telekinesis or the ability to become invisible. Others were adept healers or, like Lilith, could read minds and see the future.

Past tense, she reminded herself.

Still, exposing the presence of such power could put a lot of people in danger—especially the person she told.

"Not all life-changing experiences have to be negative," Lilith insisted, startled when the elevator dinged and the doors slid open. She really was going to have to get used to operating without her sixth sense.

"That's a mighty optimistic thing for you to say," Josie replied, joining her on the lift.

Lilith punched the L button. "Are you implying that I'm a pessimist?"

Josie pursed her lips. "You're certainly not an optimist. You kind of skirt the line."

"Story of my life."

"Is that why you're going to see Mac? Some sort of danger thing?"

Lilith couldn't argue that returning to the scene of the crime of her affair with Mac was likely not the smartest thing to do. But helping him find this drug shipment might boost her karma just enough to get the Council to reconsider their declaration and restore her powers. Besides, she intended to show Mac how she'd survived his callous rejection. She was still sexy. Still irresistible.

And he couldn't have her.

"Let's just call it extreme dating," Lilith declared, "only without the date."

"Sounds more like extreme teasing."

"Works for me."

They reached the lobby, but Josie didn't exit after the doors sliced open. "Do you want to hear about my dream or not?"

"Got a hot date tonight?" Lilith asked.

"You know I don't," Josie snapped.

Actually, she didn't know, but why quibble?

"Well, now you do. Have a date. With me. I'll bring the tequila and you bring the dreams."

"I don't drink tequila," Josie shouted as Lilith pushed her way out of the apartment building and into the sultry Chicago-in-August afternoon.

"Good! More for me."

And she had a feeling that after this encounter she was going to need every last drop.

2

HE COULD FEEL HER EYES. As slowly and as nonchalantly as possible, Mac peeled his back off the one-way mirror, certain Lilith had arrived and was on the other side of the deceptive glass. Close. With her palm pressed against the barrier. Her warmth, her spiced perfume, permeated the window with no more effort than a wisp of smoke through a screen.

He'd made a colossal mistake in calling her.

But he couldn't turn back now.

"Look, man, I don't know what you're talking about," Pogo Goins insisted, his eyes redder and droopier than they had been four hours ago when he'd come in. Goins was coming down off his high, which to Mac was both good and bad. On one hand, a little clarity on his part might help him keep his facts straight. On the other, good old Pogo might soon be lucid enough to figure out they had no reason to hold him and he had no reason to answer their questions. "I just want my ride back, got it?"

The interrogation—now being run by Rick and his partner, Det. Barbara Walters, with Mac observing in the background—had been going on for nearly an hour. Why Pogo hadn't called for his attorney yet, Mac couldn't begin to guess. Likely because they hadn't accused him of anything. In fact, they'd catered to the guy, bringing him all the cigarettes and doughnuts necessary to appease a serious hangover. They'd shot the shit since this morning, stringing him along with leads on his beloved stolen vehicle. But criminals came in two types: those smart enough to keep their traps shut until their lawyers showed up and those stupid enough to think they could deal with the cops without legal counsel. He could only hope that Pogo fell into the second group today.

Technically Pogo hadn't done anything wrong. This time. He simply had information—possibly information he didn't even know he had.

They'd had a tip.

Nothing more than a vague inference.

Which was why they had to proceed with caution.

Which was why Mac had called Lilith.

Which was why he was heading to Flanagan's on the River right after work for a stiff drink.

"My, my, don't you look delicious from behind."

Mac nearly swung around, but he held steady. He was wearing an earpiece, but even the mechanical device couldn't dull the intensity of Lilith's sultry voice.

She even wolf-whistled. She nearly deafened his left ear.

He stretched his hands into his blazer pockets, somewhat obstructing her view of his ass. What he couldn't do was respond. If Goins got even a hint that Mac was taking help from the other side of the one-way, the interview would be over.

"Mr. Goins," he said, alerting his detectives to the fact that Lilith had arrived, "I'm real sorry that your car got jacked and that you've been here so long. I know you've given us all the information you can recall."

God, he hated playing good cop.

"Yeah, yeah," Goins replied. "I mean, the snacks and cigs have rocked, but I think maybe I need to get going, you know?"

"He's nervous," Lilith said.

No shit.

"We've really been trying to cut down on the petty crimes in your area," Mac said. "I mean, guy like you, on the straight and narrow for, what, a year now?"

Goins nodded, his greasy hair swiping along the sides of his razor-sharp cheeks. "I'm clean, man. You can ask my PO. Nothing dirty on me…nothing dirty around me."

"You know he's lying, right?" Lilith interjected. "This is boring. And it's hot in here. Why don't you take off your jacket? I could take off my blouse. It'll be fun."

He was going to kill her.

"We know you've been clean, Pogo," Mac reassured, attempting to ignore the instantaneous image of a bare-breasted Lilith, licking her lips lasciviously, anticipating the strike of pleasure she'd experience when he took her nipples into his mouth. Moisture swelled on his tongue. He swallowed hard. With conviction.

Conviction. Yeah. Cop word. Remind him of the job. Of the point of calling Lilith in the first place.

Though Pogo had been more relaxed with the other detectives, Mac couldn't ask Rick or Barbara to plug in with Lilith. Not because he feared she'd tease them mercilessly with her nonstop sexual suggestions, but because he was skirting all kinds of protocols by using a psychic in the first place, especially for a case that had little to bolster it except one vague tip. If anyone got heat from the chief or the new mayor for bringing a civilian into the investigation, it would be him.

Mac patted Pogo on the shoulder. "We know you're one of

the good guys now, Pogo. Word is out you're not in the game anymore. That's why we're all pissed about this punk stealing your ride. Here you are trying to get your life back together and you lose your transportation to work. Where are you working again?"

Pogo's crooked front teeth chewed on his scarred bottom lip. "I'm driving trucks. For my cousin."

Barbara tilted her head to the side, her bright blue eyes sparkling with just enough feminine interest to mask the not-so-subtle crinkle of her nose. "Which cousin is that again?"

"Larry. He's got six rigs. Small stuff. But he makes clean money, okay? Nothing shady."

"He's telling the truth about Larry," Lilith interjected. "But he's nervous. The word *trucks* got him. Fish in that direction, hot stuff. See what you can catch."

The "hot stuff" notwithstanding, at last Lilith had offered something useful. Maybe the cousin, Larry, was on the up-and-up, but someone else in the operation possibly wasn't.

"Is that where your car got jacked? At the truck yard?"

Goins swallowed deeply.

Lilith whistled softly. "Ooh, that one registered on the Richter scale. Have you ever noticed that the word *jacked* is sexy? Why is that?"

Mac growled.

Lilith sighed. "Keep going back to the car."

"We've got to establish scene of the crime, right?" Mac asked. "You look a little nervous. You don't have to be nervous, Pogo. You're here just as a citizen who has been victimized by a growing criminal element. But we can't help you if you don't tell us the whole truth."

"Can you blame him, boss?" Rick offered, taking the tack

of—what?—*better* cop to Mac's good cop? The way they'd all been catering to this criminal lowlife made Mac's stomach turn, but the ends simply had to justify the means. "Mr. Goins has been in here as a suspect. Probably doesn't trust us. I mean, if I were him, I wouldn't trust us."

In Mac's ear, Lilith cursed. Instinctively Mac's neck jerked, but Goins's suddenly sullen expression kept him steady. Mac watched the man's lips pull tight across his teeth, and when he shook his head, sweat dripped off the stringy strands of his hair. Mac expected Lilith to break in with some sort of insight, though he hoped she'd keep strictly to business. He didn't know why he bothered with such an unrealistic expectation. The sound of her voice, coupled with her sexy commentary, were playing cruel tricks on his body. She'd always had a knack for banter that ping-ponged between serious insight and naughty suggestions—suggestions she'd make good on once they were alone.

Mac's mouth instantaneously watered in anticipation.

Damn Pavlovian response.

Yet this time she remained silent.

"Come on, Pogo," Mac urged, leaning on the cold metal table separating the petty thief and low-level former drug dealer from his detectives. "Tell us where you really were."

"I was at a bar, okay?"

"Where?"

He gave the location, a hole-in-the-wall with a less-than-reputable clientele.

Rick scooted back his chair, the legs screeching on the tile floor. "You told us earlier you were at the grocery."

"I was there before. I just went to grab a beer before going home. There's no law against that. Someone must have followed me."

"Someone like who?" Barbara asked, her blue eyes narrowing. In her late fifties, she was the top female detective in the department and was especially effective in interrogation, though she and Goins went back so far that any trust between them had been broken long ago. That was the trouble with Goins. He knew practically every cop in the precinct, thanks to his less-than-honest ways. He was particularly hard to trip up, despite his obvious hangover, simply because he'd been in enough interrogations to teach a class at the academy.

"Look, Pogo," Mac broke in. "We just want to help you find your ride, but now your story is changing on us. Where were you? Shopping for milk and eggs or club hopping with that new squeeze of yours?"

Goins rolled his eyes. "Yeah, do I look like the type bouncers are going to let in some club? I just went in for a brew."

And overheard something?

Where was Lilith? Mac glanced at the window. He couldn't see anything, of course. Had she taken off?

Mac considered slipping out for a minute, but Goins seemed on the verge of telling them something. He had to ride this out.

"But you got more than a beer while you were there, didn't you?" Barbara asked.

Goins pushed back from the table. "I don't know what you're talking about, man. I just want my car."

"There. That's it, Mac. Go in for the…"

Mac didn't have a chance to respond when the door to the interrogation room slammed open. The minute he saw the tacky diamond ring on the intruder's left hand, Mac knew the interview was over.

Shit. Why hadn't Lilith warned him?

And now what the hell was he going to do?

TORTURE. PURE TORTURE. It was bad enough when Mac faced her, flashing her with glimpses of his deep maple-brown eyes, stubbled square jaw and lips that curved just enough to be delicious and manly at the same time. But when he'd spent the interview with his back to her, she'd had an unhampered, uninterrupted view of his amazingly tight ass. An ass she'd once adored with her mouth and hands in unadulterated appreciation. An ass she craved even now. Damn him.

She sipped her hot drink, brewed with the chamomile tea bag she'd swiped from Det. Walters's desk. Barbara didn't seem to mind Lilith's continued petty thefts. One of these days Lilith was going to replace what she'd taken. That ought to be good for an extra-credit karma point.

But first she had to concentrate.

Okay, she couldn't read Goins's mind. When she'd had her psychic powers, she could plug into most people's thoughts as if she had a listening device implanted in their brain. With more sophisticated liars, her psychic vision had allowed her to see images—pictures, sometimes even words spelled out in block letters—which she'd had to then interpret into the information she needed. Oftentimes, the interpretation had been the hardest part of the experience. Only after years of training with her aunt Marion—the witch from whom she'd inherited her power—had she learned how to block out all the detritus and focus only on the information she sought. Now when she focused, her screen was blank.

But the stirring in the pit of her stomach that alerted her when someone was lying still seemed to work.

And Goins had her feeling as if she needed a huge dose of Tums.

Having Mac so close and yet so far wasn't helping matters either.

She pressed her fingers against the glass and tried to focus on the subject of the interview. She closed her eyes instinctively, but when she did, the roiling in her stomach ceased. She forced her eyes open. Good goddess, she was going to have to relearn how to do everything. Back when she'd been a child, before she'd grown fully into her power of clairvoyance, she'd suffered endlessly from an upset stomach. Not until her mother had caught her chugging Mylanta had she learned that her physical reaction to lies had been strong enough to sicken her. Her mother, filled with guilt and remorse, had then—and only then—sat her down and explained that Lilith was a witch of sacred gifts and that someday she'd hold sway over those around her because of her abilities.

God, how old had she been?

The sick feeling returned, and not because of mistruths. Only a few months later Amber St. Lyon had died, leaving Regina and Lilith to discover their magic alone. Okay, not alone. Aunt Marion had been there, as well as the rest of the Council, all of them keenly aware that the scope of power passed down through the St. Lyon line required that the girls be groomed and molded with precise care. They'd done a hell of a job with Regina, who'd taken over as Guardian on her sixteenth birthday, the youngest witch in two centuries to assume such a lofty position. With Lilith…well, suffice it to say that by the time she was sixteen, she could control her power…and little else.

"Well, well, if it isn't the Chicago Police Department's resident soothsayer."

Lilith spun around, cursing at being caught off guard yet again. She sharpened her four-letter words from mildly offensive to shockingly harsh when she recognized who'd called her out.

Boothe Thompson.

"That would make you the criminal element's equivalent of Santa Claus, wouldn't it?" she snapped.

Boothe smoothed his manicured hands down the length of his tailored Italian suit. "I'm much too slender for that comparison, Lilith, don't you think?"

She raised an eyebrow. "When exactly did we get on a first-name basis?"

"I find it hypocritical to trade insults with someone and then address them formally. And I may be a lot of things, but hypocrite is not one of them."

"No, I suppose being a bottom-feeding ambulance chaser takes up way too much time for anything else," she retorted and then added, "Mr. Thompson."

His lips curved into a half smile. "You are the feisty one, aren't you?"

Lilith stepped forward, inwardly cursing at how she could read nothing from this man. And not because of her lost powers. From the first minute she'd crossed paths with this infamous defense attorney over a year ago she'd been unable to read him. She sometimes ran into mundanes—nonmagical mortals—who could effectively block her psychic abilities. She figured a scum-bucket attorney like Boothe Thompson had honed his truth-masking abilities from an early age. She experienced the same effect with some stage-trained actors and, not surprisingly, experienced boutique saleswomen. Particularly those who worked on commission.

"The feisty one? Compared to whom?"

"All charlatans of your ilk," he replied, sneering. "How the mayor allows his department to employ frauds and swindlers like you is beyond me."

Lilith rolled her eyes. "I expect there's quite a bit that's beyond you. Like the fact that I'm the real deal."

He stepped closer. "Is that so? Tell me, then, *Ms*. St. Lyon…" he said, emphasizing the *miz* sound so that he nearly hissed like a snake. "What does your third eye reveal when you look at me?"

Lilith squared her shoulders and, despite her lack of magical powers, stared into his steel-gray gaze with bold rebellion. She concentrated but saw nothing. Not so much as a flicker. And the sick feeling in her stomach had nothing to do with lies. Pure feminine instinct turned the juices in her belly into hydrochloric acid.

"I see a handsome, arrogant man who believes he holds sway over every man and woman within a fifty-foot radius," she answered.

Boothe frowned. "Only fifty feet? You seriously underestimate my ambitions."

She bit the inside of her mouth to keep from smiling. His overconfidence struck her as funny somehow. Probably because in a way it mirrored her own.

"Perhaps. But you like to keep your friends close and your enemies closer. You work in small, concentrated bursts, luring people to your side, confident that even when they're out of your sight they'll still love and adore you."

His eyes brightened. "Perhaps you're not the fraud I suspected you to be."

She didn't reply. A few short days ago, she would have

gloated, knowing her abilities were as real as the diamond on his left ring finger. Now all she could rely on were her feminine instincts. But with a guy like Boothe Thompson— slick, attractive and precision-oiled—she had insights to spare.

"You, on the other hand, are all smoke and mirrors," she concluded.

He chuckled, raised his hand to…what? Pat her cheek? Her fingers coiled into a fist, but he stopped before his skin touched hers when he caught sight of the action on the other side of the one-way.

"Now that isn't good."

Lilith spun around and caught the fearful look in Pogo's eyes. She pushed herself away from Thompson and reestablished the connection to Mac.

"There. That's it, Mac. Go in for the…"

The door to the interrogation room slammed open.

Instantaneously her earpiece exploded with dueling shouts from Mac and Boothe Thompson.

Game over.

She yanked the listening device from her ear and wondered how one filled out a job application. Judging by her non-magical performance as a psychic, she needed a new profession. Soon. Very, very soon.

3

MAC PEEKED ONE EYE OPEN, then immediately pressed his lids tight. "Go away, Lilith."

He heard her close the door. Her stiletto heels clicked across the terrazzo floor but stopped their ominous tattoo when she reached the edge of his desk. A desk he liked in an office he liked—all courtesy of a job he liked. A job he'd devoted his life to since trading his college degree in criminology and four years' service in the military police for a badge emblazoned with the City of Chicago's official seal.

A job he might have been kissing goodbye right now if the chief of police didn't owe him for saving his life once.

"So got any ass left for me?" Lilith asked.

Mac shifted uncomfortably in his seat and opened one eye halfway. "Let's just say it's a miracle I'm sitting."

"Chief chewed off all that prime meat?"

"And spit it out right in my face."

She leaned forward on her hands, her green eyes twinkling with carnal knowledge. "Then I'm glad I had a chance to check your butt out earlier, before there was nothing left to see."

"I thought you hated my guts."

She snickered. "Takes too much energy to hate. It's much more fun to hang around the people you're pissed at and make their lives miserable."

The tease in her voice should have annoyed him, but Lilith's laugh never failed to remind him that life wasn't over just because some perp got off or the new mayor was using Mac to show the rest of the force what a tough guy he was. Or that a woman he once thought he loved believed him to be an asshole.

Not that he blamed her. He'd acted like a first-class bastard when he'd realized she possessed a power he couldn't wrap his just-the-facts mind around. Even now, resentment burbled in his belly because she'd used her natural advantages to coil him tightly around her finger. He'd been blindsided by her true abilities, even though she'd assured him from the start that her powers were real.

But when the truth had finally sunk in, he'd said things no man should ever say to a woman. His guilt was lessened only by the fact that she'd shot back with venom of her own— venom that stung. Venom he'd deserved.

Mac crossed his arms over his chest and balanced his heels on the stack of reports he should complete within the hour.

"Well, you've succeeded. I'm officially miserable. Is that why you didn't warn me Boothe Thompson was about to blow my interrogation?" he asked, ignoring how delectable she looked in skintight, painted-on jeans and one of those flimsy blouses that made no secret of the curves underneath.

She stood her ground. "Didn't know it was my day to keep defense attorneys from doing their jobs."

"Pogo Goins never asked for his attorney."

"Then why was Thompson at the precinct?"

Mac shrugged. "Followed an ambulance in? I forgot to ask."

"Yeah, you were too busy assaulting him," she replied, and not surprisingly, he heard no chastisement in her voice.

Except for criminal types, anyone with a brain knew in less than ten minutes that Boothe Thompson was a creep.

"Well, it's one way to relieve stress," he said.

She pushed Mac's feet aside and settled onto the corner of his desk, her feet dangling in impossibly sexy high-heeled boots. "Not to mention end a career. What exactly happened in the chief's office? Beyond the rending of gluteus flesh."

Mac kicked off his desk, rolling backward in his chair before her increasingly alluring scent stole his ability to think. The exotic spices counteracted the effects of the aspirin he'd choked down in anticipation of writing the report of the incident that had left Boothe Thompson with a bruise on his chin and Mac with his ass in a sling.

"Same old warnings and ultimatums," he replied. The lie tasted natural on his tongue, which worried him even more.

"You suspended?"

"Not yet."

"Do you expect to be?"

This time her voice had sharpened with the sound of outrage. Great. Just what he needed. A loudmouthed ex-lover who would relish a chance to march into the chief of police's office and give him a piece of her mind on Mac's behalf. Or maybe she'd make sure his possible suspension turned into a permanent firing. With Lilith, he never could tell.

"Look, it's been a kick seeing you again, and if not for the interruption, your help might have scored us the information we needed, but I have to get this newly flattened backside to work while I still have a job. I'm sure you have…I don't know…palms to read somewhere."

"That's the best thank you I'm going to get, isn't it?" she asked. "And for the last time, I'm out of business."

"Then maybe we'll soon finally have something in common," he replied. He grabbed the corner of the report and tugged, but the paper didn't budge, securely held down by her curvaceous backside—a backside she gave him a delicious view of when she shifted to release his paperwork.

Her mouth, so sensually shaped and enhanced by her dark burgundy lip gloss, dropped open. "Something in common beyond an insatiable need for hot, sweaty sex?"

Despite the instantaneous spike in his temperature, Mac snorted. "We don't even have that anymore."

"That was your decision," she responded, taking the opportunity at their proximity to slide her dark-red-tipped finger across the path from the monogrammed police logo on his polo shirt to the base of his throat.

"You gave me no choice," he said, gazing straight into her eyes, daring her to contradict him.

As if she needed a dare.

"You always have a choice."

He leaned closer and instinctively breathed in the scents he'd forever associate with the red sheer curtains, silk sheets and gold satin pillows of her bedroom. "Did you have a choice to be a psychic?"

She pressed her lips tightly together. "At first, no."

His mouth dried. "And now?"

Her lip quirked up, bringing the tiny scar on her cheek into sharp relief against her ivory skin. "I'm working on it."

When a jolt of hope shot through him, Mac stepped back. This relationship could not be renewed. Not when he and Lilith were so diametrically opposed in every aspect of their lives they might as well have hailed from different planets. "What does that mean?"

In a quick move, she stood and charged toward the door. "Never mind. Look, don't call me again, okay? I'm not the w-woman I used to be. I can't help you anymore."

Mac narrowed his gaze. He might not have psychic powers, but he'd managed enough interrogations to know when someone he'd once been close to was both uncomfortable with the subject matter and…lying? Lilith? She broke rules, defied conventions and generally caused consternation among any group that demanded adherence to a certain code of behavior, but she never lied.

At least not to him. With him she'd always told him the truth. Unfortunately what he'd chosen to believe of that truth had ultimately caused the destruction of their affair.

"Lilith, what aren't you telling me?"

She stopped at the door, startled. "I'm not telling you a whole hell of a lot. You see, when you call a girl a freak and then bolt out of her bed as if the sheets are on fire, you pretty much lose your right to be a confidant."

Ouch.

"I deserve that," he admitted.

"Damn straight you do!"

"I'm sorry."

Lilith opened her mouth, stopped, then popped her lips closed.

Mac shoved his hands into his pockets. Those words, hard as they were to say, were woefully overdue.

For a split second her gaze softened. But before she could respond, his office door banged open, nearly knocking her against the wall.

"What the fu—"

The mayor, the newly elected Perkins Dafoe, gave her a

quick and startled glance, then dismissed her. Okay. So she didn't exactly look like a typical voter. Not with that bloodred lipstick and pentagram charm dangling between her generous breasts. But Lilith didn't cotton to blatant disrespect.

Oh, the man was going to be sorry.

"Mancusi, what the hell kind of operation are you running here? This is the twenty-first century, man. Al Capone and Eliot Ness no longer work here."

Mac pressed his lips together to smother a smile when Lilith muttered, "What a moron."

The mayor turned toward her again, his eyes narrowed. "Excuse me?"

Lilith's grin could have cut glass. "Capone never worked here. He was the criminal. And Ness was a fed, not Chicago PD."

The mayor's face was stone until his bushy salt-and-pepper eyebrow cocked over keen blue eyes. "And you are?"

Lilith stepped fully into the man's personal space. "A friend of the detective's who doesn't appreciate being run over by politicians on power trips."

Yeah, this was helping.

Mac cleared his throat. "And what can I do for you, Mr. Mayor?"

With reluctance, Dafoe turned away from Lilith. "You can pack up your things," the politician declared.

"What?" Lilith yelped.

Mac held up his hand. "Mr. Mayor, I was told by the chief that the matter would be adequately reviewed before any action was taken."

"One look at Boothe Thompson's face is all the review I need. You're out of here. Two weeks. Maybe more if I hear one whiff of you interfering in any police matters during your suspension. I can't have my police officers beating up on my defense attorneys."

"I had no idea you personally owned the justice system of Chicago," Mac retorted.

Dafoe's bloated face reddened. "This is a new administration, Mancusi. An iron fist is what I promised my constituents, and that's exactly what I'm going to provide."

Mac's throat burned from the exertion of keeping his mouth shut. He'd walked right into this one. Common sense had told him to let Goins go when it was clear the information he may or may not have possessed wasn't forthcoming. Instead he'd called Lilith and pushed the boundaries of good police work.

But it still stank.

"There's still a shipment of drugs out there, Mr. Mayor. The distribution could be transpiring as we speak."

The mayor's jaw tightened. "That's no longer your concern."

Lilith grabbed the mayor's sleeve and spun him around. Mac couldn't react fast enough. Not with the desk in the way. A split second later, a security guard had Lilith's face pressed against the wall, her arms tight behind her back.

"Back off, you oaf!" she demanded, striking backward with her head and knocking the guard in the chin.

"Lilith…" Mac warned, his body burning from the inside out in his efforts to remain still. The last thing any of them needed was a free-for-all. Especially when more than one person in the room was armed.

The mayor had been shuttled to a corner by his handlers. Through the dark sleeves, he could see the man's sweaty face.

"Call off your man," Mac insisted.

The mayor stuttered, "Sh-she attacked m-me!"

"I barely touched your arm. Boy, won't the press love to know how you react when a woman merely touches you? Your wife must be so—"

"Lilith," Mac said, his volume low and his tone dire.

Surprisingly Lilith quieted, the obvious insult to the mayor's masculinity hanging heavy and acrid in the air.

Mac turned to the mayor, whose skin had turned the color of boiled beets. "I'll pack up my stuff with no comment to the press if you allow…Ms. St. Lyon…to leave, as well."

Two aides whispered in the mayor's ear. He nodded.

"No comments to the press from her either?" the aide verified.

Mac waited for Lilith to agree. After a tense minute, her eyes widened in surprise. "Oh, am I allowed to speak now?" She twisted so she could eye the security guard still holding her tightly. He made no move to release her. With a sigh, she agreed to the terms.

The aides shuttled to the door. The mayor straightened his jacket, then marched out behind them, stopping at the threshold. Once certain his security guard had planted himself directly between Lilith and the politician, he cleared his throat to speak, punctuating his words with jabs of his finger. "Not a word from you, Detective Mancusi. If one quote appears in black and white attributed to either you, your representatives or this…this…woman…you'll turn in your badge for good."

With that, he left. Ten seconds later, the room cleared out entirely. And yet Lilith remained by the door. Almost immediately her naturally pale skin went entirely white. Mac vaulted around his desk to catch her before her knees buckled.

"Lilith?"

Her lids drooped over her stunning eyes but didn't entirely

close. He was immediately struck by the scent of her perfume and the spiked fringe of her hair striking against his neck like a thousand matchsticks. She kicked her feet and shook her hands, mumbling unintelligibly. Whatever had come over her, she was fighting to remain conscious.

With a curse, he lifted her into his arms just in time for her to mutter, "Holy sensory overload," against his cheek.

"You're joking?" he snapped. "This is a joke?"

She groaned. "No…joke. Put…me…"

The demand trailed away. He set her down in the nearest chair, pressing his palm against her clammy cheek. "Are you sick? Should I call someone?"

Lilith shook her head gingerly. "No," she insisted, pushing him aside. "Give me a minute."

Mac backed away, realizing after he had some distance that his chest was sore from the pounding of his heart. "What are you doing, Lilith? Trying to manipulate me the old-fashioned way now that you've quit being a psychic?"

She'd put her head between her knees but looked up slowly and with pure poison in her eyes.

"You're kidding, right? I just got manhandled by the mayor's goons and you think I'm playing a game? I'm not used to relying on my normal senses. Smell. Touch. Look, I'm not going to bore you with all the details, but suffice it to say that adjusting to life without my—"

She stopped and flopped back down into the crash position.

"Without your what?"

"Without my common sense, apparently," she snapped.

Mac took a deep breath and turned to the storage closet, digging around until he found a box whose contents—a collection of ball caps from the department team—he dumped uncivilized—uncemeoniously onto the floor. Forget her. She wasn't part of his life anymore. He'd saved her from arrest for assaulting a public official, but now that she was safe, he simply had to give her a few minutes to get her equilibrium back after being nearly choked by the mayor's muscle and then she could leave. And he could leave. They could both leave and be done with the insanity that had been their relationship.

Not to mention the sudden craziness of his job.

"You're just going to give in?" she asked the minute he shoved the ashtray crafted by his six-year-old niece into the box.

"She lives!"

She sat back in the chair, the soft pink color in her cheeks slowly returning, and shot him the finger.

"Disappointed?" she asked.

"I never wished you ill, Lilith. I just wanted you out of my life."

"Then why'd you call me this morning?"

He grabbed a commendation off the wall and shoved it into the box. "I was trying to stop a crime wave. That's what usually happens after some drug lord dumps a couple of hundred kilos of powder on the streets."

"Do you always put the requirements of your job ahead of your personal needs?"

"Do you really need to ask that question?"

Lilith pressed her hand to her roiling stomach and realized she was going to have to either get used to interacting with people without her power to anticipate their every thought and action or she would have to hole up in her apartment until the Council came to their senses. Since the chances of that happening were closer to none rather than slim, she figured she'd better start acclimating herself to a new, psychic-free life.

"Do I have a choice?" she muttered. "I can't read you anymore, Mac. If I want to know what you're thinking, I have to ask."

He shoved a stack of files and a date book into the burgeoning box. "But I don't have to answer."

Touché.

"What about the police union?"

Mac pawed through a drawer, looking for…what? Knick-knacks? Mementos? Forgotten packs of gum? Lilith didn't have to be psychic to know that he wanted his files. His notes. His cases. Cases that would turn to ice the minute he walked out the door. "They'll advise me to take the temporary suspension in lieu of assault charges."

"Thompson could still have you charged," she reminded him.

"Are you going to try and beat him up for me, too?"

Lilith smiled at the thought, but she wasn't much of a scrapper. She left the big physical confrontations to her sister and her handy-dandy energy bursts.

"The mayor's a wuss. I really was only trying to get his attention."

"Well, you definitely succeeded."

"Score one for the home team," she cracked.

"Thompson told the chief he wouldn't file charges," Mac told her. "I'm guessing he wanted to buy a chance at my cooperation at a later date."

"Oh, yeah. You're a real quid-pro-quo kind of guy," she said snarkily, knowing that to Mac, a game of tit for tat was as appealing as a being the lead-in pitcher for a Little League team playing against the White Sox.

And that was the problem, wasn't it? She did know Mac. As she'd known no other man in her entire life. Their affair had started off as a lark, an act of surrender to a lust so powerful even her psyche had been overwhelmed. Though she'd never admit it, she'd employed her powers in ways she never had before. She'd wanted to be his dream woman. She'd wanted to become a part of his life, a segment of his soul. The connection between them had been inescapable until he'd torn away from her so brutally. Why was she back again? For more punishment?

Or to undo her past mistakes?

"Go home, Lilith," Mac insisted. "Thanks for trying to help out, but I don't think I need your services anymore."

She slid her slim fingers onto her not-so-slim hips, a smile tugging at her insides. At the core of her belief system, Lilith accepted that everything happened for a reason. Her meeting Mac. Their affair. His discovery of her powers. Their dramatic breakup. The stripping of her powers by the Council. His phone call earlier. The confrontation with Boothe Thompson. Mac's run-in with the mayor and his suspension.

She'd come to the precinct today in an attempt to prove her worthiness to the Council. Maybe, just maybe, she could prove something to Mac instead.

And even to herself.

"You said you didn't need me three months ago," she said. "And yet here I am."

Her voice had gone all sultry, deep and husky, and Mac's body responded. His chin tightened. His pupils dilated. His nostrils flared.

"Yes, here you are."

She swept closer to him, knowing that the fragrance she wore—one Josie had created just for her—never failed to intensify whatever emotions Mac felt toward her. Anger. Curiosity. Lust. Especially lust. Just because she'd had her powers stripped didn't mean she couldn't use someone else's magic to get what she wanted.

Namely, Mac.

Another chance to do things right.

He clenched his fists at his sides. "Lilith, you and me…we aren't a good idea."

Lilith took one of his hands in hers and eased the tension from his fingers. Long fingers. Skilled fingers. Fingers she wanted to feel in her hair, on her breasts, between her legs.

"Then let's be a bad idea. Come on, Mac. You've had one hell of a day." She slid her hands around his neck, groaning at the powerful feel of his muscles against her flesh. "What have you got to lose?"

4

"MY MIND?"

And yet, when Lilith moved toward the door, throwing him a saucy look over her shoulder, Mac grabbed his box and followed. The tension that had drawn them together months ago on the missing-child case still tugged at him with relentless power. And, God, he was too tired to fight. Thanks to this second fit of uncontrolled temper, his entire future as a cop was in jeopardy. And worse, a shipment of drugs that could turn the ebb and flow of crime in the city into a killer tsunami was likely even now flooding onto the streets. And there was nothing he could do to stop it. Nothing.

So why resist what could be at least a few hours of blissful sensation while his world drowned?

When Rick stopped him in the hallway to insist they review a case before he left, Mac handed over his badge and his gun, then blew him off. He'd call him later. Chicago wasn't going to morph into Sodom or Gomorrah before quitting time. The cases could wait. Mac's common sense could wait. Everything could wait.

Everything except Lilith.

Once they were in the shadowed parking garage, Lilith eased her backside gingerly against his car, a 1970 Ford

Mustang Boss 302. The car's need for restoration never screamed for attention as much as it did with Lilith's sleek lines and bold colors contrasting against the Mustang's rusted bumper and peeling racing stripes. Instantaneously an image flashed in his mind. Lilith in the same pose, with the same innocent expression, staring at him intently while the sales rep from the auction talked him into buying the car despite the fact that he didn't have the time or the extra cash to fix it up. But now, as then, she'd looked too alluring leaning against her automotive equivalent—fast, powerful, in complete control of whatever road she drove—for him to resist.

He dropped his box, his arms shaking.

She quirked an eyebrow. "Slippery fingers? I hope you haven't lost your touch," she purred.

He crossed his arms tightly over his chest, fully aware of his protective stance. "Are you doing this?"

"Doing what? Turning you on?" She wriggled her backside against the faded metal. "I sure hope so."

He shook his head, his gut gurgling from the emptiness in his stomach. "No…I mean, yeah. Are you, you know… making me feel this way?"

Anger churned his insides. Mac could forgive Lilith for just about anything but not for manipulating him again. Not with her…powers. Not if he was unable to fight her.

Her chuckle was devoid of its usual lighthearted rumble. "I told you, I—"

"Chose to stop using your power to make a living. I get that. But—"

"No," she said, her voice firm and just a little bit sad, a sound that caught him unaware. Lilith wore many emotions on her sleeve, but sadness was one she kept carefully contained. "I don't have my abilities anymore, Mac, and it wasn't my choice. My powers are gone. They've been stripped out of me the way a surgeon would cut out a spleen. Or a heart. You could be thinking right now that you want to strangle me with your bare hands and I wouldn't have a clue."

And this wasn't insignificant. Once Mac had accepted that Lilith's psychic abilities had been genuine, he'd figured out so much about her. Why she didn't carry a cell phone but always seemed to know when someone needed to talk to her. Why she hardly glanced around her when she exited the L but still managed to thwart the thief who once tried to grab her jewelry. She relied on her heightened intuition to ensure her connection to the world and her safety. Suddenly it occurred to him that she wouldn't give up her abilities without a fight.

Someone had cut them out of her. Against her will. But who? And why?

"What happened?"

"Long story," she responded, her eyes averting and her fingers toying with the silky edge of her blouse.

He lifted the box back into his arms. "That's convenient since I recently acquired more free time than I know what to do with."

Tension seeped out of her shoulders when she licked her lips. "I know precisely what to do with all that free time, if you'll stop being afraid of me."

"I was never afraid of you."

A burst of laughter echoed in the deserted parking garage. "I distinctly remember terror in your eyes the minute you realized that I could read your thoughts."

He shifted uncomfortably. She was right. He had been scared. All his years in law enforcement, both in the military and walking the beat, he'd seen a hell of a lot of freakish stuff.

He'd even run across a few situations that seemed completely
unexplainable. But never in his life had Mac considered that
the forces at work were beyond the ordinary. Ghosts, to him,
were manifestations of people with vivid imaginations. Practitioners of voodoo or Santeria scared their followers into
submission with lots of goat's blood and manipulative place-
ment of slaughtered sacrifices.

Yet when Lilith had proved her abilities to be very real, he'd
been totally unprepared. She'd told him precisely what he was
thinking—word for word—with images and visualizations he
knew no one could guess at. She'd picked his brain open like
a safecracker and cleared the contents without breaking a sweat.
He'd freaked out, reacting from pure, basic fear of the unknown.

"Then how about if I say I'm not afraid of you anymore."

She shrugged. "I lost my powers. You don't need to be."

He narrowed his gaze, searching for some sign that she
wasn't being straight with him. Not that she'd ever earned his
distrust, but once a cop, always a cop.

"So you can't manipulate me now. You can't *make* me
want you."

She ran her hands through her hair, then laced her long and
sensual fingers behind her neck, causing her breasts to jut tempt-
ingly. "I never could. Read your thoughts, yes, but put them in
your head? I wish. I could never make you want anything, Mac,
not the way you think. Well, not using *those* powers anyway."

A tightening that spawned in his chest dipped decidedly
lower. "What other kind of magic do you have?"

Her smile instantly allayed his residual fear. "Relax,
Mancusi. I'm talking about the kind of magic all women
possess. There's nothing supernatural about you wanting me
now. In fact, I'd be damn worried about you if you didn't."

She held out her hand, then with a coy glance over her shoulder indicated precisely what she wanted. Instinctively he tossed her the keys. Though he wasn't entirely sure that she had a driver's license, Lilith's unexplainable adoration for his car spawned his habit of always allowing her to drive. When the metal hit her palm, she squealed with delight, immediately unlocked the driver's-side door and slid inside.

The popping of the trunk acted like a starting pistol. He tossed the box of his memories into the back and spun around to the passenger's side just in time to see her lean slinkily across to let him in.

"Where are we going?" he asked.

"Is that another way of saying *My place or yours?* Those really are the only two choices, you know."

Mac was about to agree when another car eased by behind them. A Lamborghini Murcielago Roadster. Silver. Expensive. And driven by none other than Boothe Thompson— with Pogo Goins riding shotgun. Mac couldn't ignore a unique opportunity. Sure, he was off the force. And, yeah, he'd been ordered by the mayor to leave all of his open cases alone. But how could he bypass such a perfect opportunity to find out exactly why a high-priced mouthpiece like Thompson was fronting for a lowlife like Goins?

"Speak of the devils," Lilith muttered.

Mac turned toward her, his face blank. He could only wonder....

"You want to follow him?" she said.

He frowned. "I thought you lost your psychic ability."

She rolled her eyes impatiently. "A girl doesn't have to be psychic to figure out what you want to do, Mac. I mean, if I were you…"

He slid into the passenger seat. "You'd make a great cop."

She turned the key in the ignition. "I'd suck as a cop and you know it. No matter how I try—and, frankly, I don't try, very hard or very often—I can't manage to follow rules."

With a quick glance over her shoulder, Lilith eased out of the parking space, then maneuvered down the row just as the tail end of Boothe Thompson's car dipped down the ramp.

"I've followed rules my entire life," Mac lamented, "and look where it's gotten me."

Lilith didn't reply, concentrating instead on pursuing their quarry at a stealthy distance, reinforcing Mac's suggestion that she'd make a decent police officer. Psychic or not, Lilith was a street-smart woman, and if she possessed even a modicum of fear, she kept the emotion skillfully hidden. He wouldn't take this risk with any other civilian in the car, much less driving. Besides, they were just following someone. He didn't anticipate any danger to anyone but himself, since stalking charges didn't look good on the chief of detectives job evaluation. If Thompson made him and complained to the mayor, his suspension would become permanent.

Unaffected by the potential consequences, Lilith clucked her tongue but continued to pursue the Roadster at a safe but tight distance. "I'm corrupting you," she said without the least bit of remorse.

"Maybe it's about time."

The light at the corner changed to red, trapping Thompson's car at the intersection. Lilith used the delay to turn toward him completely.

"Damn, Mancusi. Just when I thought I was over you, you go and do something that's got me melting inside. Putting your job on the line. Disobeying orders. Breaking laws."

Even with the rumbling of the engine and the vibration of the overstressed metal beneath the stripped leather seats, Mac heard her breath switch from normal aspiration to tiny little pants. The green rings of her irises tightened into strips of intense color.

"Bad boys turn you on?" he asked, realizing for the first time that he knew little, if anything, about her sexual past. Beyond him, of course. Beyond assurances of safe-sex practices, neither one of them had shared many details about previous lovers. Their relationship, such that it was, had left little time for conversation.

"On occasion," she confessed haughtily. "But if you want to really get me wet, it's the good guys gone bad who do the trick."

Before he could stop himself, Mac grabbed the back of her head, yanked her close and kissed her hard. The jolt of electricity that shot through his body nearly sent his heart into cardiac arrest. She tasted like honey and tea and woman. She smelled of melted candle wax and fragrant herbs. Her tongue battled with his, fighting for dominance, yielding only after he slipped his fingers into her hair and teased the tips of her earlobes with his thumbs. She whimpered, acquiesced, then retaliated by splaying her palms over his chest and pressing hard against his beating heart. His muscles bunched and ached as he fought from pulling her out of the driver's seat and onto his lap.

But no matter how much he wanted to make love to Lilith and lose himself in the hot, familiar sex they'd once shared so freely, the honk from the car behind them reminded them that they had a more pressing goal.

With a look that promised more at the soonest opportunity, Lilith jumped back behind the wheel and threw the car into gear. They'd lost some ground on Thompson, but thanks to rush-hour Chicago traffic, they hadn't fallen too far behind.

The rest of the trip transpired in relative silence, with Mac breaking the thick quiet with quick instructions that Lilith deftly followed. They arrived at the South Side neighborhood unseen. Surrounded by the common props of industrial blight—overturned garbage cans, one shuttered door or window for every visible pane of glass, loiterers on the street who ranged in age from about fourteen to eighty but who all shared a common distaste for hygiene—Mac's battered car blended in.

Lilith slid the Mustang into a space in front of a Laundromat, while Boothe double-parked across the street in front of a dingy bar whose only glitter came from a score of flickering neon signs.

The Lamborghini gleamed amid all the dust and grime, yet none of the people on the street seemed to stare or ogle the vehicle. A few, however, stepped quickly away.

Boothe got out of the car, his step springy as he engaged the security alarm, which Mac figured had to be the type that shut down the engine at unauthorized entrance or else Thompson would never park in this neighborhood. Of course, a shut-off switch wasn't going to stop someone from relieving him of his state-of-the-art car stereo or any other sellable items stored in the vehicle.

In contrast to the attorney, who acted as if he walked these mean streets every day, Goins had his hands shoved deep in his pockets and his head buried in his upturned collar despite the late-summer heat.

"Hmm, if you drove a pimped ride like his, would you leave it alone, illegally parked, in this neighborhood?" Lilith asked.

Mac's mind whizzed with a dozen scenarios, each as unlikely as the next, as to why Boothe Thompson would drive Pogo Goins home, much less join him in some dive bar for a drink. The same dive bar that was the last known location of Goins's stolen car.

"Seems to me that Thompson knows his ride is safe here, where Goins's wasn't. And do you notice anything about the locals?"

Lilith took her time, leaning forward and then back. "They don't seem to think that a three-hundred-thousand-dollar car on their street is anything unusual. Which means…?"

"Mr. Thompson is a fixture."

"He is a defense attorney. I'd venture to guess that there are a lot of people around here who need defending."

"Yeah, by fee-free public defenders, not attorneys who import their cars, their suits, their shoes and their jewelry from Italy."

"How do you know that ring is from Italy?" she asked, curious.

He tapped his temple with his finger. "Logic, deduction and intense police work."

She smirked. "He bragged about it, didn't he?"

Mac matched her sardonic grin with one of his own. "Maybe. Once. Boothe Thompson isn't the kind of guy who wants to blend into the woodwork."

"Hence his sharing a brew with a guy whose entire net worth is less than the cost of Thompson's haircut."

"Precisely."

Mac unbuckled his seat belt and opened the car door. Lilith moved to do the same, but he stopped her. "Whoa, there, hot stuff. I broke enough rules letting you tail the guy. As a civilian, you stay in the car."

She skewed him with a bored expression, then proceeded to do what she wanted to anyway. "If that's the case, you need to get that fine ass of yours back in the car, too. Remember? You're among mortals now, too."

The irony struck Lilith powerfully, but she fought her reaction and instead concentrated on scoping out her surroundings, something she'd never really had to do before her psychic abilities had been stripped away. Like Mac, she'd lost the one thing she'd depended on her entire life to define who she was. For her, it was her magic. In his case, his position of authority. In her many forays into his mind, she'd witnessed scenes of six-year-old Mac lecturing his two-year-old brother and three-year-old cousin on the proper way to engage their G.I. Joes in action. She'd seen glimpses of him captaining his football team with strictness that rivaled the hard-assed coach. His service in the military had struck her most deeply. He'd had the lives of his men in his hands, and instead of fearing his responsibilities, the authority had empowered him.

Too bad she had to defy him now. She couldn't prove a thing to the Council about her ability to sacrifice for others and act selflessly if she sat in the car, now could she?

Luckily he didn't argue. She locked the car door and tossed him the keys. Mac popped the trunk, dug out a crappy old jacket from underneath his box and shrugged into it, lifting the hood over his head in a way that made him look like a stalker or the Unabomber—and also ensured that he fit right in with the locals. He grabbed a moldy, holey sweater and held it toward her.

She sneered. "Not in this lifetime, Mancusi."

"You want everyone noticing you?"

"They'll notice me no matter what bag lady costume you

try to put on me," she said, smoothing her hand over her hip. "It's a curse."

He chuckled. "Tell me about it."

Abandoning the trunk, he went into the backseat and pulled out his own bomber-style leather jacket. One thing about Chicagoites—they never went far without a collection of outerwear, even if the weather, like today's, bordered on balmy.

She shrugged into his jacket and inhaled the intoxicating scents of tanned animal skin and male musk. Only a few days ago, such sensory overload would have jolted her with a flash of premonition. Instead she experienced a dizzying infiltration of memory—her own—of wearing this jacket and nothing else after Mac had spent the night on a stakeout. They'd made love in the courtyard of his apartment building, then again on the stairs. The mating had been much like the jacket itself— carefully made, warm and hinting of age and experience.

The recollection made her shiver.

"You okay?" he asked, his eyes glinting as if he knew precisely what she was thinking about.

She quirked a grin. "I'd be better if we were crushing the hibiscus again rather than following two creeps into a crappy bar."

He bit his lip and, if she wasn't mistaken, blushed before he turned back toward the street. "So would I."

They waited for a delivery truck to squeeze around the Lamborghini, then used the massive vehicle as cover to cross the street unseen. For all they knew, Boothe had positioned himself next to one of the blackened windows. Wouldn't the defense attorney have a field day reporting back to the mayor that a detective who had lost his badge and a civilian with a questionable reputation were tailing him?

They slipped into an alley next to the bar, nearly tripping over a guy napping in a cardboard box.

"How do we play this?" she asked as they picked their way through the garbage cans to the side-door entrance to the bar. "Boothe Thompson isn't stupid."

Mac tested the doorknob, rolling his eyes when it opened without protest. "I'm counting on this joint being anything but a clean, well-lighted place. Add to it the clouds of cigarette smoke and we should be fine."

Though Lilith doubted the bar served more than peanuts or stale chips with their well drinks and less-than-premium beers, the kitchen smelled like rotted cabbage and rancid grease. Just beyond the door, a stereo blared, unbalanced to favor the bass, with hard-metal riffs that would effectively drown out any conversations transpiring within. Lilith held her nose as they scurried through the kitchen like the rats that clearly lived among the torn cardboard boxes and grimy crates. Mac opened the swinging door into the bar a few inches, spotted Boothe Thompson sitting near the back, then grabbed Lilith's hand and hauled her inside.

She nearly choked from the stench of tobacco and unwashed bodies, suddenly craving the sweet celery and woodsy cedar that dominated her altar in her quest for healing. Mac dragged her into a booth, gestured to the bartender for two beers and pulled the hood of his jacket closer to his face.

"Can you see Thompson?" he asked.

Lilith leaned three inches to her left. Her view, blocked by a pole, cleared. "I can see Goins. He doesn't look happy to be here. He's sucking down his beer as if the world supply of hops is running out."

Mac's face reflected his confusion. "Thompson has his back to the door?"

Lilith nodded, then realized she was in the same position. A wave of discomfort rolled over her and she couldn't stop the instinct to glance furtively over her shoulder. Suddenly her awareness of her loss of power spiked again as it had in Mac's office after the attack of the mayor's goon. The smoke seemed to thicken, press in on her. Every different smell, from sweaty skin to cheap cologne, assaulted her. Every sound of every voice shoved into her ears. When the bartender banged two cloudy mugs on the table, she yelped.

Mac slid across his seat, blocking any view of her from behind them. He tossed a five onto the table, and the bartender, who glared at Lilith oddly, immediately snatched the cash and disappeared.

"What was that?" he asked, his tone as hushed as the loud music would allow.

"This place gives me the creeps," she admitted.

"You're not usually this jumpy."

She wasn't usually so aware of her powerlessness.

"I don't make it my business to hang out in bars that don't wash their glassware. Ever," she replied, sliding the spotty mug away from her.

Mac lifted his brew and took a long swig. "Sometimes you have to take risks."

Lilith couldn't fight the smile tugging at her lips. Venturing out of her apartment nowadays was a huge risk without her psychic abilities to act as a shield. Of course, she did have Mac, who seemed more than up for the task.

"What do we do now?" she asked.

Mac frowned. "I shouldn't have dragged you into this."

"Woulda, coulda, shoulda," she said, slipping her hand over his and toying with the rough skin on his knuckles. "Regrets suck, Mac. I'm here. I'm resourceful. Let's make this interesting."

5

JOSIE POKED HER HEAD through the doorway, peering through the wild collection of personalities crunched into the police precinct. Not surprisingly, she caught more cases of the shivers from the guys in uniform than from the criminals in handcuffs. She couldn't believe she'd come here. The sensation of her morphing into red meat in a den full of hungry lions was hard to shake, but on Lilith's behalf, she had to try.

Seeing no sign of dark, spiky hair, sheer blouse or anyone else remotely resembling her friend, Josie fingered the lapis lazuli charm she'd put on this afternoon because it matched her blue skirt—the very necklace Lilith had given her from her own collection simply because she'd admired it. When the cool blue gem had touched her skin, an overwhelming need to find Lilith had struck her with a vengeance. Though Josie's primary talents were in the use of herbs and scents for aromatherapy, candles and potions, she knew enough about premonition to never ignore such a strong feeling. Not when a friend might be in harm's way.

Shifting from foot to foot, she bolstered her courage by remembering that, cop or not, Mac Mancusi had been a cool guy. Sure, he'd looked at her funny when they'd first met—but all men pretty much did that once they caught sight of the thin beaded braid she wore down the side of her face, her tie-dyed blouses, bangle jewelry and Birkenstocks. Once they spied the pentagram tattoo on the back of her neck, men generally ran for the hills. Well, the kind of men she liked, anyway. Handsome. Intelligent. Self-supporting.

Normal.

Such preferences kept her alone. A lot.

"May I help you?"

Josie jumped, hitting her shoulder on the doorjamb. As she rubbed the sore spot and turned, she was flattened by the most beautiful brown eyes she'd ever seen on a man. At least since her dream.

"Sorry," he said, his grin sheepish, his voice melodiously deep and accented. His teeth practically glistened against his dark skin. He smelled of sandalwood and the heavy, dry scent of leather, topped with a hint of citrus. Lemon, to be exact. The combination sparked an instant image of hot sex in the great outdoors.

"Are you okay?" he asked.

Josie opened her mouth to speak but couldn't manage to form any words. Was he the man from her dream? The masculine presence she'd felt so strongly, but hadn't actually seen?

This was too weird, she thought, frowning.

His grin disintegrated from welcoming to suspicious.

"Are you looking for someone?"

Josie closed her eyes, sought and found her balance. She breathed through her mouth, determined not to be waylaid by this man's choice of cologne.

"Mac," she recited, her lids still tightly shut. "Mac Mancusi."

When she peeked open an eye, the man's suspicions had clearly deepened. He crossed his arms over his chest and widened his stance. The black strap of his shoulder holster flashed from beneath his lapel, reminding her of who he was and where she was.

She laced her fingers into her skirt.

"Do you know Detective Mancusi?" he asked.

"Yes. Well, sort of. He used to be involved with a friend of mine. Well, he is again. I think. Look, she might be in trouble and she told me she was coming here and…"

His expression hardened as she babbled, from his eyes to the set of his mouth. She stopped talking and pressed her lips tightly together. Embarrassment quickly gave way to anger. She should have known better than to come here and expect even a modicum of consideration and respect from men in uniform—even if he wasn't literally wearing blues, but instead a surprisingly well-fitted suit. Still, cops were all alike. And now that she was no longer blinded by this guy's pearly whites, sexy eyes and melodic voice, she could see that her best bet was to take off and try to find Lilith somewhere else.

"Thanks for all your help," she said before darting around him.

He grabbed her gently by the arm. She gasped and nearly stomped his foot, but he immediately released her.

That's all she needed—*another* charge of assaulting a police officer. She'd been a juvie the last time, and the cop had been manhandling her—not that anyone had believed her side of the story. But they'd purged her record, right?

"Sorry. Are you looking for Lilith St. Lyon?"

Josie couldn't help but glance down at her arm. Her skin tingled. Not a prickly, cold tingle but a warm tickle of a vibration that burrowed deep into her body. Just as she'd felt last night in her dream.

She shook her head, willing sense to override her libido. "You know Lilith?"

The detective shrugged, his shoulders undulating underneath the very nicely fitted suit jacket. "We've worked together. I was the one who suggested she be brought on this case this morning." His volume dropped. "I don't know if Mancusi is ever going to let me forget it, either."

"Did something happen to Lilith?"

"She's fine. I assume."

Josie slammed her hands onto her hips. "You know what happens to people who assume."

"What is that?" he challenged.

She arched a brow. "Do I have to spell it out?"

"Lilith can take care of herself," he replied defensively.

"And you know this how?"

"She's with Mac," he responded, his tone final.

Ordinarily Josie might have shared this guy's assessment that Mac and Lilith had more than enough resources between the two of them to remain safe and sound in just about any situation. But she couldn't ignore the premonition. Not when she'd never gotten one before.

Maybe her feeling of foreboding hadn't been about Lilith but about Mac. Of course, that didn't make any sense. She barely knew the man. But then, her having a premonition at all was about as unusual and unexpected as her showing up willingly in a police station.

"I need to speak with Mac right away."

"He's gone."

"Can you contact him somehow?"

"He's out of touch."

"When will he be back?"

The detective's frown spoke volumes. "Not for a while. A long while."

That didn't sound good.

"What happened?"

"Look, it's a long story," he replied. Then, as if his emotions could glide on ice, his mouth curved back into that devastating smile. "And one he'd probably prefer I not go spreading around to beautiful women, especially ones who haven't told me their name yet."

Handsome and charming? And a cop. How could she be so…lucky? She supposed she could give him her name. It's not as though she had any outstanding warrants. At least none that she knew of. "Josie Vargas. And you are?"

"Vargas? That's…"

"My father's Peruvian," she said, and this time it was her turn to cross her arms over her chest. Being blond and blue-eyed often brought odd stares from other Latinos, especially those with the classic dark hair, skin and eyes.

But instead of surprise, his smile was warm and welcoming, causing a shot of guilt to spiral up her esophagus…and a jolt of attraction to shimmy down her spine.

"Rick Fernandez," he answered, his accent coming through loud and clear this time. "My family's from Miami, originally Cuba."

Okay, so they had something in common—a heritage tied to the Spanish subjugation of the New World. Didn't mean she had to trust the guy. He was still wearing a badge somewhere in the vicinity of that gun.

"You must love the winters here," she cracked.

He chuckled, the sound deep and rumbling. Like an oncoming avalanche.

"I've been here six years. I think I know all the best ways for keeping warm." His tone had dipped with innuendo.

She smirked.

"Am I coming on too strong?" he asked, his head humbly tilted downward.

She laughed despite her best efforts not to. Josie had a long history of making questionable decisions when it came to men. She couldn't afford to add flirting with a cop to the list. Not without introducing the distinct possibility of getting burned. Again.

"Can you help me find Mac or not?"

"He took off with Lilith." He took a few steps away from the squad room and invited her closer with a nod of his head. "He got suspended this afternoon. Lost his temper. Hit a defense attorney."

Josie's mouth dropped open. "And here I thought he was Mr. By-The-Book."

"Every man has his breaking point."

And with Lilith around, Mac probably crossed his with growing frequency. But Josie understood better than anyone how Lilith could be attracted to a man who was her polar opposite. Mac was a rule maker. Lilith rarely acknowledged that rules existed. Of course, Josie wasn't one to cast stones. She had this crazy thing for normal guys with jobs that paid FICA while she'd never worked for anyone but herself her whole life.

"So you have no way to contact him?" she asked, trying to ignore her instinct to steal one more whiff of Det. Fernandez's cologne.

He took a step closer. Damn him. "I called his cell a few minutes ago and he's not answering."

She eased a few steps backward. "Well, that sucks."

"Is there a reason you need to see him? Maybe something I can help you with?"

Again the vibrations in his voice added a timbre of seduction to his tone, as if the "help" he was offering had something to do with hot kisses and sweaty sheets. Man, it had been too long since she'd gotten laid.

"Not unless you know some way to find him and Lilith as soon as possible. I think they might be in danger."

Rick blew out a frustrated breath, dug his hands in his pockets and started to move away. Then he stopped, turned slowly, a grin that was pure, unadulterated wickedness breaking his face into a contrasting study of dark and light.

"Well, there is *one* way."

She pursed her lips. There was no mistaking the naughtiness in his tone this time around. "Am I going to like this 'one way'?"

He held out his hand and winked. "Depends. Do you believe in magic?"

LILITH BIT HER BOTTOM LIP, waiting for Mac to respond, watching how his eyes betrayed the conflicts raging through him. Clearly he wanted her help. Needed it, actually. And as much as this liability pissed him off, he wasn't a stupid man. Passing up her offer to spy on Boothe Thompson for him could mean a singular opportunity missed—and Mac wasn't one to turn away from that knock on the door. Not when the public safety—as well as his career—was on the line.

"I need to know what they're talking about," he admitted. "If Thompson's in collusion with Goins, if he knows something about that drug shipment, he could be disbarred. Talk about a shift in favor of law enforcement."

Lilith squelched the instinct to pump her fist victoriously. "I'm more than ready for the task, but I'm going to have to move in closer."

Mac scowled. "He'll recognize us."

Lilith peered around the column again. Thompson still had his back to them. Goins, while facing in their direction, didn't seem interested in anything but his beer and whatever Thompson was telling him. "They'd both recognize *you,* yeah, but only Thompson would recognize me and he can't see us. I know Goins from interrogations, but he's never actually seen me. This is perfect."

Lilith started scooting out of the booth, snagging her jeans on the ripped vinyl. She was twisting to check out the damage when Mac grabbed her wrist.

Electricity jolted through her and she couldn't contain the heat surging through her veins. She could still taste his kiss. His eyes reflected that same raw need. Then, he'd acted on pure sexual desire. Now that she was willing to help him with this case he had no business working on, the emotion shifted to something more. Something familiar. Something terrifying.

Even without her powers, she could feel the healing between them. The sheer force of his fear for her, in the midst of her magical powerlessness, simmered her blood. She could do this. Even without her clairvoyance. For the first time in days, she spied a glimmer of light to what had been a literal and figurative psychic darkness.

"You're not getting all nervous on me, are you, Mancusi?" she asked teasingly. "All I have to do is listen in. You're ten feet away. What kind of trouble could I possibly get into?"

He arched a brow. Both of them knew perfectly well that Lilith could get herself into trouble in a locked and padded room.

"Don't get too close," he warned. "If you run into trouble, scream. I'll launch myself over the crowd in a split second. But I can't risk turning around and spying on you. If Goins makes me, he'll bolt and we'll never find out what he knows."

"Or what Thompson knows."

Mac nodded, his jaw tight. Must have been a huge shock to his system to realize that a man like Boothe Thompson, top of his field, was mixed up with someone as potentially unsavory as Pogo Goins. Lilith, on the other hand, had no trouble wrapping her mind around a defense attorney getting his hands dirty with the scumbags he represented. Such was the way of the world.

She lifted her wrist, still encircled by his hand, and swiped a kiss over his fingers. "You worry too much."

Lilith diverted first to the bar, where she ordered and received a bottled brew. After swiping the want ads from on top of the jukebox, she strolled leisurely to the booth directly behind Thompson and slid into the seat.

"You need to calm down, Goins," Thompson said, his voice calm but authoritative.

"Man, it's like he was reading my mind, you know? He nearly got me to spill. I was so wasted."

"Which explains why you went to the cops in the first place. They're not about helping guys like you, Pogo. Not with problems like this. You do realize that if the cops had found your car, they'd have access to everything in it? Next time you have concerns, you come to me."

A shiver ran through Lilith's blood, and she had no discernable reason for the response except that Boothe Thompson's voice seemed edged with something deeply sinister—or was she simply forcing judgments because she couldn't read him? Still, Lilith may have been without her powers, but she hadn't lost her life experiences. Boothe Thompson was not one of the good guys.

"Thanks, Mr. T," Goins responded, slurping his beer noisily.

"Please, Pogo. Outside the court system, it's perfectly acceptable for you to use my first name. I was just saying the very same thing to my friend, Ms. Lilith St. Lyon, not two hours ago."

Lilith didn't move. Had he spotted her or was he making idle conversation?

"Who?" Goins asked.

Lilith turned the page on the paper quietly and, hopefully, casually.

"The woman who was helping Detective Mancusi with your interview."

"Nah, that's Walters. She busted me last year for possession and intent to distribute."

"Not the detective in the room. The undeniably attractive woman listening in. The one with the seemingly insatiable need to eavesdrop on conversations that are none of her concern."

Okay, she'd been tagged. Lilith took her time folding her pilfered newspaper, then glanced over her shoulder, not surprised to find Boothe Thompson grinning at her slyly.

"What gave me away?" she asked.

He leaned closer over the back of the booth and inhaled deeply. "Your scent is incredibly…unique. Unforgettable, even. I'd say patchouli oil is the base. With white musk, black currant and—" he took a deep breath "—sandalwood. An almost male fragrance, actually, but decidedly feminine on you."

Lilith smoothed her tongue over her teeth, giving her a chance to think before she responded. She pushed out of her mind the question of why some guy knew so much about scents and focused on the situation at hand. First and foremost, she didn't want to alert Mac. His charging to the rescue could buy him more trouble than he could afford. Boothe Thompson, despite his assurances otherwise, could still press charges against Mac for their earlier altercation, which could effectively end her former lover's career as a top cop.

She had to throw Boothe Thompson off her scent—literally and figuratively. With no other power at her disposal, Lilith decided to play to his obvious flirtation.

"I'll tell my perfumer you approve."

Boothe returned her smile, though his expression bordered on arrogantly indulgent. "You might want to have him design a different scent next time you go on a reconnaissance mission for the Chicago Police Department."

Lilith snorted. "My perfumer is a she, but you obviously have the wrong impression about our chance meeting."

She kept her voice down. The music was loud, but she figured Mac was doing everything he could to listen. She didn't dare flick so much as a quick glance in his direction for fear she'd give him away. Like it or not, Boothe Thompson was holding all the cards right now, including the one that could trump Mac's career.

"So little in this world happens by chance. Why else would a woman like you come in a dive like this except with ulterior motives?"

"I could ask the same question—changing the gender reference, of course."

"Mr. Goins chose this establishment."

She leaned over and peered at Goins, who was sweating profusely. Damn, if only she had her powers. This guy would be as easy to read as the back of a cereal box.

He slurped his beer, then stuttered, "The beer's cold."

Lilith lifted her bottle. "That it is."

"Now that we all agree on the chilled temperatures of the beverages, I believe we should go back to the original topic of why you are here." Thompson turned, leaning sideways against the wall so that he had Lilith in full view—and Mac in partial view. If the cop turned around, he'd be spotted.

Lilith scooted out of the booth. Beer in hand and want ads tucked beneath her arm, she swung around and sat next to Goins, who had the decency to move over after Lilith bumped him with her hip. "Funny, I was under the impression that a defense attorney of such repute would understand the whole freedom-of-movement thing we have in this country. I can go wherever I want whenever I want. Isn't it great how that works?"

Goins nodded enthusiastically, but Boothe's icy eyes merely narrowed.

"You don't find it coincidental that we'd end up at the same establishment after the dramatics that occurred at the police station?" he asked.

She knocked back a long swallow of beer. "I find it hugely coincidental. But the way my luck's been working lately, I'm not surprised."

"You looking for a gig?" Goins asked, spying the newspaper seconds after she slid it onto the table.

She nodded.

Thompson eyed her boldly. Clearly her ruse of using the classifieds as a cover wasn't fooling him for a minute. "This isn't exactly the job-search capital of the world."

"Really?" she asked, sticking to her story if for no other reason than to annoy the bastard. "Where exactly should an out-of-work psychic go? I hadn't heard that the big shots in the Loop were looking for a little extrasensory help to determine future stock prices."

"That would be illegal," Thompson noted.

"Only if the psychic was legit. I got the distinct impression a few hours ago that you believed I was a fake."

Fingering his beer mug but putting none of the bitter brew in his mouth, Thompson chuckled. "Speaking of believing, I believe that you followed me here from the police station. I believe that your very intimate friend, Detective Mancusi, sent you here to eavesdrop on my private, protected-by-law conversation with Mr. Goins." He scooted closer and the color in his eyes seemed to darken as malice swirled in the icy depths. His hand shot across the table, flattening his strong fingers over Lilith's, trapping her. "I believe that the detective sent you into a very precarious situation."

Rage boiled inside Lilith, but she used every ounce of her self-control to keep her emotions in check. If she made one move that signaled a threat, she knew Mac would launch himself into the fray without a second thought to his career. Instead she sat up straighter, jutted her breasts and when Thompson took obligatory notice, she chanced a glance across the room at Mac.

He was watching. Turned to the side with his collar pulled up high, no one else would ever have noticed he was there. And he was staying put despite the fact that Thompson had his slimy hands on her. Another woman might have been offended by his lack of protectiveness, but Lilith's confidence expanded in her chest like a deep breath. If he didn't think she could handle the heat, he would have run to her rescue.

But she could handle Thompson. Him and anyone else who wanted to mess with her. Power or no power.

She yanked her hand away, then turned to Pogo Goins. "You know, if you came clean to the cops about why your car was really stolen, you'd be a real hero."

Goins snorted. "A real dead hero."

The veins on Thompson's temples quickly and painfully expanded. "Pogo, as your attorney, I advise you to say nothing more."

For every degree that Thompson's face reddened, Pogo's face paled. The attorney's advice was sound, but his tone glistened like the edge of a newly whetted blade. As the two men engaged in a charged battle of stares, Lilith chanced another glance at Mac.

He was gone.

She searched the crowd frantically, hoping he wasn't on his way over. The animosity between Thompson and Goins could be used, if they could separate the two. Goins was terrified, but he clearly knew more than he'd admitted.

"Looking for someone?" Thompson asked, his voice venomous.

"The friend I was meeting here."

"Let me guess. This friend is about six foot two, two hundred heavily muscled pounds, dark hair, dark eyes, olive skin, Italian heritage...."

"Jeez, don't quit your day job," a female voice said the minute she popped out of the crowd.

Lilith grinned from ear to ear at Josie's sudden appearance. "He wouldn't make it in the psychic biz, would he?"

Josie scrunched up her nose and looked Thompson over. "Not without a turban, a dashiki and a television show on public access."

As Thompson scowled, Lilith couldn't help but laugh.

Just picturing a smooth operator like Boothe Thompson in such an incongruous getup was enough to cause a serious fit of the giggles.

Josie grinned happily, then held out her hand to Lilith. "So I was thinking…. This place has tons of atmosphere and all, but what do you say we head over to Navy Pier and check out the kiosks. I'm thinking that's the way we want to go with our new venture."

Lilith slapped her hand on the table. Josie's amazing interruption couldn't have been better timed. "It's been a pleasure, boys."

Goins chugged the rest of his beer while Thompson glared. As she turned and followed Josie out of the bar, Lilith wasn't exactly sure what she'd accomplished on her reconnaissance mission except to alert Thompson's suspicions and confirm that Pogo Goins possessed information—something tied to his car, possibly—that could get him killed. She supposed that was a start.

Though sunset was just an hour away, the light outside blinded her as they pushed their way to the sidewalk. Out of the corner of her eye she watched Josie give a wave, then lead Lilith across the street to where the Mustang was parked. Josie tossed her the keys.

"I heard you have a thing for this car," Josie said.

Lilith slid behind the wheel and waited for Josie to join her at shotgun. "I have a thing for the guy who owns it."

Josie's eyes widened.

A deep male voice chuckled from the backseat. "Isn't that good to know."

6

LILITH TURNED AND leveled Josie with a deadly stare.

"Did I forget to mention that Mac's in the backseat?" Josie asked innocently. "Rick just took off. He'll meet us at home."

Lilith shook her head wearily and pulled the car into the street, fighting the temptation to bang right into Boothe Thompson's Lamborghini on their way out. Not only would she get the satisfaction of ruining Thompson's pretentious car, but she'd give both Mac and Josie a jolt they both deserved.

"Having fun back there?" Lilith quipped, swerving at the last minute to give the Roadster a safe berth.

Mac chuckled. "Just keeping out of sight until we're at the corner."

Annoyed, Lilith failed to slow down at the stop sign, so Mac was forced to remain in his less-than-comfortable position for at least one more block. Wasn't much by way of retribution for his hearing her confession, but it was the best she could do on short notice. Once he unfolded his large body from off the floor, he leaned over the seat, his mouth dangerously close to Lilith's ear. "So tell me more about this *thing*."

She stopped grinding her teeth long enough to shift into third gear. The car lurched forward, but he held tight to the seat.

"I think it's called insanity," she replied.

"So you have a *thing* for me," he repeated, emphasizing the word in an arrogant tone that made her want to smack the smile off his face…or kiss him silly, she wasn't sure which. "It's not like you've revealed any big secret."

No, she hadn't exactly been hiding her attraction to him. But to Lilith, saying "a thing" privately to her one and only close female friend implied a hell of a lot more than Mac clearly understood. As a guy, he likely equated "a thing" with "the hots." Well, duh. She'd gone out of her way today to make sure Mac knew that she was still as sexy as ever and that if he wanted a taste or two of what he'd walked away from, she was more than willing to serve herself up. Wasn't as if she would lose out in the deal.

But as she shifted the car into fourth and sped onto the interstate, she wondered if she could really walk away from a fling with Mac unscathed. She thought she had last time— and, boy, had she thought wrong.

Wasn't that she'd been in love with him and he'd broken her heart. She couldn't love a man who refused to accept her for who and what she was. But she cared about him. The first time he called, she put her ass on the line for him, attempting to nail a drug-dealing perp without the protection of her powers. Okay, she'd done that to help herself, too, but more to help Mac, truth be told. And while the thrill of mixing it up with a slimeball like Boothe Thompson had exhilarated her, she wasn't blind to the implications of her choices. The anger she'd been harboring since her ugly breakup with Mac had melted away a lot more quickly than she was proud of. On the other hand, she relished the freedom from those overwhelming negative vibes.

And if she was completely honest with herself, her concern about Mac, his career—even this case—explained why the idea of getting him naked and in her bed as quickly as possible was as inevitable as the sun setting to the west of the Hancock Building.

They were going to be together again. It was just a matter of when and where. And how toxic the fallout once her powers were returned to her.

"What happened with Thompson?" Mac finally asked.

Traffic on 94 started to crawl, so Lilith downshifted as she recounted the conversation for him, both what she overheard and the exchange between Thompson, Goins and herself once she'd been spotted.

"They're into this drug shipment hip-deep," Mac concluded. "We need to track down that car."

Lilith smirked. She believed the same, but not because she had any hard proof. Wasn't her psychic powers either. She just could smell lies when she heard them. Felt them, actually. And her stomach was still churning from the experience. Mac, on the other hand, normally relied entirely on nothing less than irrefutable facts. Of which they had none.

"Goins is scared about some information he has—or had, if it was in the car. That much is clear," she said. "But Thompson might just be trying to protect his client."

"I don't think so," Mac responded.

She couldn't help grinning. "Why not? Suddenly psychic?"

Mac smirked. "Just gut instinct. Cops sometimes rely on that."

"Not you," she reminded him. "You're more from the Joe Friday school of detective work, remember?"

"I was," he replied, his voice suddenly softer, "until I met you."

His admission shot into the air, then hovered like a black-ops helicopter about to drop a cache of Rangers onto a field of battle. She'd changed his way of thinking? She'd changed him? Good goddess, she hadn't meant to. If he started all of a sudden listening to his instincts rather than following the dot-to-dot path of the facts, their worlds had just shifted closer together. Dangerously closer together.

"You didn't get this far as a detective by never following your gut before," she pointed out, desperate to put a little distance between them again.

Mac nodded in concession. "True, but I wasn't so aware of it until recently. Maybe I've been missing out."

"On a lot more than improved detective work," Josie mumbled, her words loud and clear in the close quarters.

As the traffic started to ease forward, Lilith flipped on the radio. A classic-rock station played softly in the background, giving her a reason to tap her fingers on the steering wheel. "So where are we heading?"

"Back to your place," Mac responded. "I've got to get you ladies home."

Josie sat with her hands primly in her lap. "Does Detective Fernandez still intend to meet us?" she asked, her tone brimming with so much nonchalant innocence Lilith thought she might gag.

"We're supposed to hook up there, yeah."

"How did you and Rick get involved in our secret mission anyway?" Lilith asked her friend.

"I went to the precinct to find you," Josie replied.

Traffic crawled to a halt again. Lilith spared Josie a surprised look. "You? At the police station? Why?"

Josie gazed dispassionately out the window. "I had a feeling you were in trouble."

Lilith frowned. "Maybe you should be the psychic." She glanced over her shoulder at Mac, who was watching her intently with dark and dangerous eyes. If you considered unbridled lust dark and dangerous. Which she did.

She bit down a smile and squeezed her legs tightly together to offset the thrill shooting through her.

"No way," Josie said, waving her hands in emphatic criss-cross motions. "People's thoughts popping into my head, visions or feelings of grave danger…I had one taste today, and you can have that headache, thanks."

"What do you mean you had a taste today? You had a premonition?"

She'd always thought Josie's "had a feeling" was a simple figure of speech. Now she wasn't so sure.

"Well, I think I might have, yeah. I was on my way to my shop when I decided to wear this—" she lifted the lapis lazuli pendant from between her breasts "—and bam! This really hot wash of sensation seemed to engulf me. I saw your face and I saw Mac. I can't explain it except I *knew* you were in trouble. This has never happened to me before, so I went to the precinct to check things out, to…I don't know…prove I was wrong, I guess. Then Detective Fernandez told me what happened and he decided it would be best if we tracked you both down."

As Josie rambled on about the clever way Rick used the video from the parking garage and the triangulation of Mac's cell phone in order to find them at the South Side bar, Lilith thought about Josie's description of her premonition. *Hot wash of sensation.* Yeah, that was pretty accurate.

But how had Josie, a mundane witch, received the premonition? The lapis lazuli necklace, while beautiful, didn't possess any particular powers that Lilith knew about—and the stone had once been hers. She couldn't remember how she'd gotten it, but she guessed it had been an impulse buy of some sort. And out of all the cops marching around the Chicago Police Department's main precinct, how had Josie bumped into the one and only detective who had the resources to find Mac when he didn't want to be found? To the casual observer, Josie had played a part in a huge.coincidence.

But Lilith didn't believe in coincidences, no matter what she'd told Thompson. She'd seen too much in her relatively short lifetime to believe that the world worked without a very precise plan.

She'd have to contact Regina. If someone else—the Council, maybe—was meddling in this game, she needed to know about it. Right away.

Once they finally arrived at Lilith and Josie's apartment building, Josie spotted Det. Fernandez a few doors down, leaning against his car.

"There he is! He was so helpful. Honestly, Mac, if he didn't have your cell phone all triangulated from when you and he did that undercover bust a few weeks ago, we never would have found you. I think he's incredibly resourceful. Thinks outside the box. But still steady. Responsible. You have to admire a man like that, don't you?"

Good goddess. Josie was babbling. Which wasn't so bad, theoretically. Josie needed a man to babble about. Deserved one, actually. But Rick? He was no more suited for Josie than she was for Mac.

Lilith liked the detective a lot, trusted him even. But while he was Josie's preferred type in every sense, from his buttoned-down oxford shirts to his large extended family, she couldn't see him falling for her friend in the same way. Rick Fernandez liked his women…normal. Grounded. Bordering on saintly. He and Lilith had once had a good laugh over the ideal wife he was looking for—a model that dated back to pre-1950s. In other words, his mother. A woman who wore dresses with pearls to vacuum her three-bedroom, two-bath house with a picket fence and a dog that didn't shed. A woman he could take home to said mama and that his sisters, both of whom had had three kids before they were anywhere close to twenty-nine, wouldn't chew up and spit out at their first meeting. His dream woman could make *arroz con pollo* in her sleep and do the salsa in three-inch heels without breaking a sweat. How could free-spirited, sandal-wearing, raised-by-law-ignoring-Wiccans-who-lived-out-of-a-van-when-they-weren't-in-jail and kind-to-a-fault Josie ever measure up?

She was about to give her friend a warning when Josie bounded out of the car and beelined for Fernandez. She brushed his arm twice as she and the detective made their way to the apartment building entrance, Josie animatedly recounting how she'd finessed Lilith out of her exaggeratedly dangerous situation. She and Mac exchanged amused glances before they locked the Mustang and joined them at the front door. Mac immediately filled Rick in on the need to find Pogo Goins's car.

"Sounds like Ms. Vargas here has the stuff to follow in your psychic footsteps," Fernandez said, sounding surprisingly excited about the prospect.

"Oh, no," Josie said. "I told Lilith I want no part of her gift. I'm glad I could help today, but from now on she can keep her psychic suggestions to herself."

"Psychic suggestions?" Mac asked.

Lilith swallowed deeply. Oh, good goddess. This was *so* not the whacked theory Mac needed to hear. "Don't exist," she said.

"Well, you don't know that for an absolute fact," Josie claimed. "I've read lots about the possibility."

Lilith fished out her key to the front door and let them all into the lobby. "I'm sure the detectives aren't interested in crackpot theories from people they'd consider extreme crackpots on first meeting."

"They don't think you're a crackpot," Josie argued.

Mac shoved his hands into his pockets. "Crackpot or not, I find this topic fascinating. Go on, Josie, please."

Lilith rolled her eyes. Fascinated, her ass.

"Well," Josie said, sounding suddenly like an expert on a phenomenon she hadn't experienced until today. "There's a belief among some psychic researchers that a particularly potent clairvoyant can send a powerful image into the mind of someone who might be susceptible to the message." When Fernandez looked confused, she elaborated. Darn her. "So, like, today…Lilith was in trouble and needed help. She might have used her psychic ability to telegraph a message to me so I could help her. That's probably what happened, Lilith, don't you think?"

Lilith was about to deliver a resounding "no" when she saw Mac's eyes harden to stone. His jaw twitched. He crossed his arms tightly over his chest and challenged her with the tilt of his head to answer Josie's question. She'd spent a good deal of time today convincing him that she couldn't actually control or influence his actions or emotions, but Josie's diatribe on a little-known and never-proved theory of psychic power had clearly undone all that she'd accomplished.

"No, I don't," she said emphatically. "I've been clairvoyant since I was a kid. And it's a gift that runs in my family.

I've never seen a psychic control another person—and, trust me, I've been in the company of the most skilled psychics in the known universe. If I had the power to influence others, my mother never would have grounded me or made me do the dishes, that's for sure."

Josie nodded earnestly, oblivious to the storm she was stirring. "Well, you were just a child then. The power likely grows with age and maturity. Besides, I don't think *control* is the right word. I totally had free will today," she said, though her insistence made her claim less than convincing, especially to Mac, whose pupils seemed to have tightened into angry, black pinpoints. "I know I could have ignored the feeling that you were in danger—and I might have if it wasn't for the fact that I'd never experienced anything so powerful before. I just had to make sure Lilith was okay. Mac, you weren't answering your phone, so I took a chance and headed to the station. It was kismet that I met up with Rick."

Surprisingly Josie managed to sound totally nonchalant in her claim. And even more shocking, Rick didn't look at all put off by the prospect that his and Josie's meeting was pre-ordained. He seemed fascinated, which only annoyed Lilith more. What was happening with this world if she couldn't predict which couples were meant to be together and which ones were destined to crash and burn?

Lilith realized then that her blood, which had held steady at an annoyed simmer since this morning, was starting to boil. She'd gone out of her way today to help Mac out when she would have much preferred to stay in her apartment, away from the overwhelming feelings of helplessness when jostled or surrounded by crowds, to sulk about the loss of her powers and her sister's betrayal. But no. She'd jumped when Mac had called, telling herself she was trying to put some ticks in the "I can use my powers for good" column when really all she'd wanted to do was see if her juices were still hot for a little Mancusi action. Well, they were.

So what was he going to do about it?

Or, better yet, what was she?

"Josie, kismet is a direct result of karma. If you think you did something to earn a meeting with Rick, then there's your answer. But it certainly wasn't the result of me sending out any psychic vibes. I don't have my powers anymore."

Josie gasped. "What? Are you blocked? I'm sure I could brew up—"

Lilith cut off her well-intentioned suggestions with a quick slice of her hand. "No, I'm not blocked. I'm not choosing to stop using my abilities and I'm not pretending not to be psychic anymore just to get back in Detective Mancusi's good graces. I'm no longer a psychic and probably never will be again. Call it kismet."

The direct result of karma. Bad karma. The kind of karma that came when a witch with sacred powers used her gift for her own personal gain.

The realization made her stomach hurt. Lilith punched the up button on the elevator, which thankfully slid open instantly. She stepped in, jabbed her floor and waited for the doors to close behind her. She held her breath, half of her hoping that no one would join her and the other half cursing Mac for leaving her alone.

Again.

His weight rocked the elevator car just as the doors slid closed. He waited until they reached her floor and the bell dinged before he spoke.

"Since when have you cared about my good graces?"

She whirled around, pushing past him, angry at herself for letting loose with her tongue so freely. For showing a vulnerability she didn't want to have, much less reveal. She'd never been one to censor herself, but maybe there were certain things that were better left unsaid. "I don't. It's a figure of speech."

He followed her to her apartment door. "A figure of speech meaning what?"

She jammed her key in the lock and nearly twisted her wrist opening her door. "Meaning I'm pissed off that my powers were taken from me, Mac. Taken. I didn't give them up willingly, so don't go thinking I sacrificed who I am in order to win you back, because I didn't. I want my powers back. I need my powers back. They're part of who I am. Without my ability to sense my surroundings, I'm flying blind. I'm trying to adapt, but I hate it. I don't know what you're thinking or feeling. I don't know when someone is behind me or wants to hurt me. It's…"

"Terrifying?"

She bit the inside of her mouth. She couldn't admit such weakness to Mac. To anyone. Regina would never be afraid like this. Never.

"It's disconcerting," she clarified. "I want to be who I am. And, damn it, I deserve a man who isn't so caught up in his own insecurities that he can't accept me!"

He charged through the door before she had a chance to slam it in his face. "Is that what you think of me? You think I'm insecure?" he asked.

She stopped her rant long enough to realize that she was slipping down a dangerous slope…right into dishonesty.

"No," she said. "I'm just angry and I'm taking it out on you."

She threw her keys on the table and plopped onto the cushions of her overstuffed red leather couch. Closing her eyes, she inhaled, relishing the scents in her apartment, the same essences she'd been longing for earlier in the bar. Slowly the dried herbs and fresh celery on her altar worked their magic, reminding her that she really did need a few minutes to commune with her sister before—well, she hoped—she and Mac settled in for the night.

Mad as she was, she still wanted him. The loss of her powers had emptied her, and more than anything in either the mundane or the witching world, she wanted to fill herself up. With Mac.

She opened her eyes to find him standing close to her altar. His hands hovered near the athame, the ceremonial knife she used to cast ritual circles. And as a letter opener. She believed in practicality.

"It's funny," he said, his voice low and somewhat nostalgic. "I never asked you anything about this stuff before."

Lilith leaned forward, her elbows on her knees. Fatigue was starting to seep into her shoulders and neck. "This 'stuff' is my belief system, Mac."

He shoved his hands deeper in his pockets. "I guess I never thought about it."

She smirked. "Well, we had other things on our minds before."

"Things?" he asked wryly.

She chuckled. "If you count body parts individually."

His laugh acted with more relaxing powers than all the potions or scented candles in Josie's store.

"Point taken. Not that you're complaining," he added.

She stood and rubbed her suddenly moist palms on the front of her jeans. "Me? Complaining? Not likely. Help yourself to whatever's in the kitchen, okay? I'll be right back."

Darting out of the room before she changed her mind and attacked him on the spot, Lilith closed her bedroom door and leaned against the cool wood. She was about to shout her sister's name when she remembered she wasn't alone. She could, of course, reach her sister via traditional means, but she was longing for a little magic in her life, even someone else's. She turned on the CD player beside her bed, slipped into the bathroom, turned on the faucet and then called Regina with the summoning incantation she'd learned as a teenager.

A couple of sparks later and Regina was standing in front of her, looking considerably less regal than the last time they'd seen each other. Dressed in yoga pants and a snug tank top and glistening with sweat, Regina had clearly been interrupted in the middle of a workout.

"What's wrong?" Regina asked.

"Other than the fact that you raped me of my powers, not much. Thanks for asking."

Regina rolled her eyes. "Don't hold back, sis. Tell me how you really feel."

Lilith opened her mouth, but her sister placed her palm over her lips to stop the free flow of complaints. She had, after all, asked for it.

"I take it back," Regina said. "I know you're angry. And you know there's nothing I can do until the Council sees that you've recognized the error of your ways."

Lilith longed to remind her sister that she hadn't done anything requiring such an extreme punishment, but Regina pressed her hand tighter. "Just tell me why you summoned me."

Unable to sigh in frustration with her mouth covered, Lilith growled. Rehashing an old argument wasn't going to accomplish anything except prolong her time away from Mac. She'd sacrificed enough for the witching world. She wasn't going to give up hot sex, too.

Responding to Lilith's glare, Regina removed her hand.

"It's Josie."

"Your friend upstairs?" Regina asked. "Is she all right?"

"Yeah, she's fine. But she received a premonition today. About me."

Regina pursed her lips.

"You did it, didn't you?"

Her sister's shrug wasn't an admission of guilt, but it was pretty darned close. "I worried that you might run into a little trouble without your powers, so I sort of set up Josie with a warning system. That way I'm technically not interfering with the lesson the Council feels you so desperately need to learn."

"So you've essentially hired someone to babysit me. I thought you gave up on chaperones when I turned twenty-one."

Regina ground her teeth audibly. "When you became an adult, I thought you had the good sense to use your powers only to help others."

"I was helping—" This time Lilith cut herself off. Regina was a member of the Council, but she wasn't the only high witch with a say in her fate. And despite Lilith's protestations to the contrary, Regina had to be on her side. Except for their aunt Marion, the two of them had been on their own for a long time, even before their mother died. As Guardian, Amber hadn't exactly been around a lot. Their sperm-donor father had lit out shortly after Lilith's birth, apparently when he realized that he wasn't going to be crowned some sort of witch king just because Mom was Guardian.

That's why Lilith had always tried to be honest with Mac.

Okay, so she hadn't exactly *explained* the whole witch thing. A guy like him could only take shocking information about his lover in small snippets. Hell, the first snippet had sent him off the deep end. If she'd revealed more about her exact level of power and the existence of high witches with sacred abilities that defied the laws of physics, he might have jumped into the Chicago River and disappeared beneath the cloudy green goop forever.

On cue, Mac's voice broke through the music and flowing water.

"Lilith?"

Regina raised an eyebrow. "Is that Detective Mancusi I hear?"

"Shut up," Lilith said before shoving Regina into the shower, slicing the curtain shut. She hurried through the bedroom to open the door just wide enough to poke her head out.

"Hey, sorry I'm taking so long."

His gaze traveled the width of her bedroom, still decorated in modern-day harem. She liked to feel pampered at the end of the day. And sexy. Mac clearly appreciated the decor more than she needed him to at the moment.

"I'm sure you'll be worth the wait," he said huskily. "I just thought I heard voices."

"You did," she admitted. "I had to call my sister."

Wasn't exactly a lie, was it?

"Everything okay?"

Lilith pressed her lips together. "No, but hopefully life will be looking up by the time you've poured us each a shot of something from my liquor cabinet. Why don't you wander over into the kitchen and find us something to munch on, too?"

Mac glanced over her shoulder. Lilith pulled the door

tighter, grinning like a moron. When he finally nodded and turned away, Lilith shut the door, scurried back to the bathroom and yanked the shower curtain open.

"Take the spell off Josie," she demanded.

Regina waved her hand.

"Done."

"Thanks. I don't want her dragged into my dramas, as I have a feeling," she said, glancing at the door, "that things are going to be…unpredictable around here for a while. And don't interfere in that, okay, Reg? I know you want me to impress the Council so that I won't embarrass you—"

"That's not—"

Lilith huffed. "—but I've got to do this my own way. Promise me, whatever happens, happens. We've grown up believing that no action in this world, nor reaction, occurs without a reason. Don't go against that now."

Regina gave a frustrated huff, then nodded in agreement. Lilith marched away from the shower, grabbed her toothbrush and proceeded to erase the stale peanut and cheap beer flavors from her mouth, not needing a hug or anything else emotional from her sister right now. After she rinsed and spit, she turned to find the shower empty. Regina had shimmered out.

Lilith had wanted her sister to leave, and yet hot moisture stung her eyes at the emptiness. How had they gotten like this? So close, and yet so far apart?

She couldn't think about that path of her life right now. Mac was in the other room, waiting for her, anticipating her appearance, wanting her as much as she wanted him. Lilith finished her primping, undoing a few buttons on her blouse to reveal the snug shell tank underneath before slipping into her bedroom to trade her boots for a pair of comfy yet sexy sandals. She considered changing into lacy lingerie but decided not to go the obvious route. Besides, before she and Mac hit the sheets, they had a few topics that needed to be discussed.

As quickly as possible.

7

MAC DRUMMED HIS FINGERS on the kitchen counter, trying not to turn around and stare at the altar in Lilith's living room. He kept himself occupied by downing another shot of the bourbon he'd found in her liquor cabinet. Had she really had an altar before? Had he really taken so little stock of the living area—as opposed to the sleeping area—of Lilith's apartment that he couldn't remember the waist-high chest covered with a blue cloth? The one holding a hand-molded ceramic bowl of sea salt, matching white-and-black candles, incense, a blossoming stalk of celery, a pentagram and a thankfully dull—and clean—knife? Clearly there was more to this woman than he'd anticipated. Other than the sex and their partnerships in the precinct, what did he really know about her?

He remembered precisely where she had her little star tattoo—a symbol he now realized meant more to her than he'd ever imagined. He remembered the exact locations of her erogenous zones, all for entirely selfish reasons. Everything else he'd thought he knew about her—from her preference for thin New York style-pizza even though they lived in the land of the deep dish to her insane knowledge of seventies rock bands and science-fiction cinema—had all become suspect when he'd realized she could read his thoughts. They'd had so much in common then. Before he knew the complete truth…that her knowledge was mostly his, gleaned from his mind by a power he'd never truly understand.

"Hey."

He started, sloshing the bottle of bourbon he held tight in his hand.

"Sorry," he said. "Didn't hear you coming."

"Welcome to my world," she quipped, grabbing the shot glass and bourbon from him.

He took a deep breath, inhaling the fresh, crisp scents of toothpaste and body spritz emanating from her body. She'd loosened the buttons on her blouse, and the way her hips made tiny figure eights while she poured bourbon into the glass testified to pent-up sexual energy. She'd made no secret that she wanted to seduce him or that she wanted to be seduced. Had his discovery of her altar and Josie's theory on psychic control changed that?

Who was he kidding?

"Want to talk about your world?" he asked, hoping she'd say no. She'd run a brush through her hair, softening the spiky ends she'd worn this afternoon. His fingers itched to weave into the dark strands. She shifted as she set the bourbon on the counter, allowing him a more enticing view of the low-cut, tight tank she wore beneath her blouse.

She downed a gulp of booze in one quick swallow, arching her back as the liquor slid down her throat. "No."

He smiled and refilled her glass. She made short work of the second shot as he poured his third. And he'd thought she only drank girlie wine coolers.

"Okay, yeah," she contradicted, smacking her lips like the

veteran drinker he'd thought she wasn't. "But we're still going to have sex, right?"

Mac's laughter belied his true intentions. Despite the alcohol, his muscles tightened. Across his chest. Around his neck. Down his back. Below the belt.

He cleared his throat to keep from choking. "That's the plan."

"Good," Lilith said decisively. "I like your plans."

"Today's plan didn't go so well."

She waved her hand dismissively. "It was off-the-cuff. As much as you think you're all 'go with the gut' now, you're really more of a step-by-step kind of guy—and there's totally nothing wrong with that. We just need more time to…strategize."

"We?"

She glanced at him seductively, and staring into her emerald-green eyes, he almost forgot what they were talking about. When she slipped the filmy blouse off her shoulders, allowing the gauzy material to flutter to the floor, he nearly forgot his name.

"Yes, we. You dragged me into this. Besides, without my powers, I have nothing else to do but work for the greater good of all Chicago. Pogo Goins knows something and Boothe Thompson is a snake. And, frankly, I wouldn't mind getting a piece of taking them down."

God, he loved how her mind worked. He loved how she talked, the way her voice dropped to sexy dulcet tones when she simmered with anger. Despite her protestations earlier, Mac knew Lilith would make a great cop. Sure, she'd spend a good deal of her time getting to know the guys at Internal Affairs or on suspension for breaking one rule or another, but when on duty, she'd make even the pettiest crime interesting.

"We may have lost our chance," Mac decided. "Maybe I

should just take a break and let the guys who still have badges handle this one. It's not like I've got a secret weapon or anything."

She crinkled her nose. "Is that a swipe?"

He winced, remembering what she'd said about losing her powers. And more than that, how she'd said it. As if her heart had been ripped out, too.

"Sorry. That was rude."

"Yes," she agreed, pouring herself another shot of bourbon, but this time disposing of the alcohol in several relatively dainty sips.

"So who…stripped…your powers?"

Lilith glanced over at her living room. Mac had been staring in that direction long enough to know she was looking at her altar. Maybe he shouldn't have asked.

"Let's just say that powers like mine don't go unchecked. If that were the case, you'd have a lot of psychics running the world, wouldn't you?"

He'd never really considered that possibility. Before Lilith, he'd never even believed true psychics existed. Wasn't easy to wrap his mind around the idea that she had to deal with psychic police. Question was, how much of her weird world spilled into his on a daily basis? Not many criminals were psychic or they wouldn't get caught. Not many cops either or the whole force would be sitting pretty with bulging jails and little to do except play poker across the squad room table.

"Clairvoyants running the world would be bad." He decided to agree with her, not knowing what else to say or what was safe to ask. Not because she wouldn't answer, but because he knew she would.

"Well, that depends entirely on your point of view," she

said with a laugh that quickly dispersed when she got back to the subject. "Anyway, the people who regulate this sort of thing decided I needed a break from my abilities. I wasn't exactly holding hard and fast to all the rules."

"You?" he asked, exaggerating shock.

She sneered, though she managed to make the ugly expression adorable. "Yeah, yeah. Big shocker. I turned my talent into a business and that didn't sit well with the…powers that be. That's why the only help I can give you on this case is the normal, backup, supportive, you-go-get-'em-Mac kind."

Mac licked his lips, enjoying the flavor of the bourbon on his skin and wanting more than anything to taste it on hers. "That's not exactly true."

Clearly she noticed the sensual intentions buried beneath his words. And happily she didn't seem to mind the innuendo.

"Okay," she agreed, biting her bottom lip. "But first you have to accept that no matter what Josie said downstairs, I can't control you. Even if I had my powers, which I don't, I could never make you feel something you didn't want to feel or do something you didn't want to do."

He slid the bottle away. "You're lying."

She stood up straight, her shoulders squared and her hands ready to wrap into tight fists. "Excuse me?"

"I just meant," he said, taking her hands in his and working out the tension with his fingers, "that whether you mean to or not, you're continually making me feel things I don't want to feel. Every minute we're together you make me do things I don't want to do. We're so different, Lilith. I'm only realizing now how far apart our worlds are. And yet here I am, wanting you, not for just an hour or a night but for—"

Her gasp silenced him.

His kiss squelched the sounds that followed.

As he'd fantasized, her mouth tasted like peppermint and smooth Kentucky whiskey served in a warm glass. Her skin, so soft beneath his touch at first, prickled as a shiver danced through her body. He pressed her close, her body flush against his. He longed to strip her bare, expose her, raw and willing, to his hungry eyes.

Before he could tear off her tank top, she pressed her hands flush against his chest and backed away.

"What?" he asked, the word tearing from his throat as if formed with jagged glass.

Her eyes glittered with what he suspected were wicked intentions. Very wicked intentions.

She reached out and ran her finger across his lips, slipping the tip inside for a split second to tease his tongue. "I made big mistakes with you before, Mac."

He shook his head to clear the lusty fog clouding his ability to process her words. "Yeah, you kept shit from me. I reacted badly. Apologized. It's over."

He reached out for her, but she dodged his grab.

"That's not what I meant." Her voice was husky, deep and hot. She sashayed a few steps away from him, her hips undulating in a dance he couldn't help but follow. "I wanted you so desperately the first time we met I changed who I was to please you, at least in the bedroom. I broke into your thoughts and stole your sexual fantasies, then made them reality."

His mouth dried as the memories swamped him. He swallowed, attempting to replenish the moisture. When it didn't work, he grabbed the bourbon and took a swig without the glass. He wiped his mouth with the back of his hand. "And the bad part of that was?"

She quirked an eyebrow, then slowly turned and strolled into the living room. His ears thrummed with the deep bass sounds of his heartbeat, suddenly in time with music about witchy women and their magical hold over their men.

Only she wasn't in possession of her powers anymore, was she? This was all her. Real and unafraid to tempt him with the rock and roll of her sweetly curved backside and coy glances over her shoulder to see if he followed.

He marched into the room just as she draped herself across the couch.

"The bad part was," she said, kicking off her sparkly sandals, "I never got any of *my* fantasies fulfilled."

Her mouth quirked into a half grin, erasing any chastisement from her tone. The past was the past. They'd both made mistakes. If Mac had thought for one minute about wanting to fulfill Lilith's fantasies, she would have read that in his mind and made sure it came to pass. Instead, he'd been having too much fun indulging his own preferences. He'd ignored hers.

Bastard.

He whipped his shirt over his head. "That's criminal."

She grinned, then curved her lips into an enticing pout. "That's what I thought. What exactly do you think is justified punishment?"

He could think of quite a collection of ways he'd like to be punished, but this retribution wasn't about him, was it? He removed his shoes and socks and, at her raised eyebrows, his slacks and boxers. Her appreciative grin worked like an aphrodisiac and his dick elongated tightly.

"Now this is a start," she said, squirming in her seat.

"Your jeans look snug," he commented, wondering if her sex was throbbing with need as much as his.

She smoothed her hands down her thighs. "Oh, yes. They're very constraining." She moved to flip open the button, then stopped. "Maybe you…"

He didn't have to be asked twice. He didn't have to be asked once, truth be told. He climbed over her, unashamed of his nudity, even as she made great show of admiring each and every inch of his nakedness.

Surprised by how her bold stare invigorated him, Mac balanced with his knees on either side of her hips and worked the fastenings on her jeans. She lifted her buttocks and he started to tug off the denim, taking her panties along for the ride.

"Uh-uh-uh," she denied, pinching the shimmering green material of her undies close to her skin so she remained covered as he whipped the jeans off her legs. "We don't have to be in a rush, do we? I mean, you're not going after Boothe Thompson tonight, are you?"

"Who?"

She chuckled as she leaned forward and indicated that he could remove her tank top, which he did with as much patience as he could muster. The material was dark, contrasting with the pale skin of her midsection and insanely arousing breasts. As he flipped the shirt over her head, his eyes immediately flashed to her nipples, but they were covered by a lacy strip of satin that matched her panties in color and insanity-inducing sexiness.

She drew one leg up, giving him a peek of dark curls clustered beneath the silk. With one lazy hand she drew soft circles over her upper thigh, frowning.

"My skin feels so dry."

He leaned forward and kissed the spot she'd stroked.

Inhaling deeply, his brain dizzied from the heady scent of her arousal. "Feels perfect to me," he said.

She slid her hand onto his cheek, tilting his head so his eyes met hers. "But I'd feel better with lotion, don't you think?"

No, he didn't. He thought she'd feel better with his sex buried deep within hers. The strain of muscle, skin and nerve endings at the center of his groin was bordering on painful, but the iniquitous gleam in her green gaze reminded him that his punishment was beyond deserved.

He stood. "Where do you keep—"

She gestured toward the bedroom.

He made short work of his search, dousing lights along the way until only the low-wattage lamp beside the couch, hot under the scarlet shade, threw pinkish beams of light across her skin. He dashed into the bathroom and tore open the medicine cabinet. He found nothing of use and turned quickly, whipping his thigh with his erection. On a small table beside the bathtub he found a basket—a treasure trove of lotions, oils and salts. He tried to pick one, but the ticking clock in his chest was too loud for him to read the labels in the dim light. Instead he grabbed the whole basket and darted back into the living room.

He stopped the minute he spotted Lilith. The contents of the basket nearly tumbled out in his haste. She'd shifted to the center of the couch, her arms draped long and lean across the back, her legs crossed daintily at the ankles. Her eyes were closed, her expression peaceful, as if she were meditating.

"Come closer," she said.

He cleared his throat. "How'd you know I was here?"

She peeked one eye open. "You know that saying about bulls in a china shop?"

He grinned. He hadn't exactly been practicing great stealth. "Put the basket on the table."

Moving the table back to give himself room, he placed the basket on the flat surface. She tapped the tabletop with her toe, indicating where she wanted him to sit.

Shifting into position, she lifted her legs, then draped them on top of his lap, her toes teasing the edge of his erection.

"Oh, yeah," she crooned. "This is perfect. What flavors and scents did you bring for us to play with?"

Flavors? Trying to ignore the sensual stroke of her big toe across his taut flesh, Mac lifted the bottles and attempted to read the labels in the relative darkness.

"The oils are all flavored and scented," Lilith informed him. "They're custom-made."

He opened the first clear bottle and undid the top, inhaling deeply.

"This one's sweet."

He leaned across, holding the cap to her nose. His shift pressed her foot full against his sex. Sensations shot through him and he nearly dropped the bottle.

She pretended to ignore how her foot was torturing him and took an elegant sniff. "That's rose. Entirely too innocent for what I have in mind."

He screwed the bottle closed and tossed it aside. Aching to smooth the oil over her skin, he opened the next bottle and breathed in before leaning forward. She rewarded his offering by stroking him long and hard with her foot. Stifling a pleasured groan nearly made his eyes water.

"That's vanilla," he said.

She smiled slyly. "I love the taste of vanilla, don't you?"

He didn't give a damn if the oil tasted like stale bread so

long as she allowed him to touch her, to tease her, to devour her nip by tiny nip. When she sat forward to inhale deeply, her nipples arched over the edge of her bra, tempting him with their tight darkness. Involuntarily he licked his lips, wishing he was licking her.

"You want this one?" he asked, ready to pour the whole damn bottle on his hands.

"No," she teased. "I want cinnamon. It's so hot and spicy yet with just a hint of sweetness."

Mac tore through the basket until he found the flavor she preferred. He popped open the top, then stopped, wondering if she had a preference on how to apply the slick emollient. He knew she did. What he didn't know was if he cared.

He did. He did care. Altar or not. Mind-reading ability or not, Mac wanted tonight to be about fulfilling Lilith's needs. She'd admitted to him that she'd made their lovemaking before all about him—which couldn't have been easy for a woman of such strong opinions and demands. But who said good lovemaking had to be easy?

Swallowing hard, he poured a tiny drop of the oil onto the tip of his finger and slicked the candy-flavored lubricant over her lips.

She took her time licking off the flavor, groaning deeply. The sound injected into his bloodstream and accelerated his heart rate to dangerous levels.

"Oh, yeah," she said. "That's the taste I want. But I want it on you. Not on me."

LILITH OPENED HER EYES in time to witness the full breadth of his shock. His brow lifted high, and the way his mouth hung open caused Lilith to chuckle. She taunted him by pressing her foot harder against his cock, loving how the curve of her arch embraced his muscled sex and how her toes teased the moistened tip.

"What do you mean?" he asked.

She shimmied her shoulders slowly, enjoying the chafe of silk against her nipples. The torment of prolonging her love-making with Mac elevated her skin temperature. Tiny beads of sweat formed in all the right places—at the baseline of her hair, beneath her breasts and between her legs, as if the eroge-nous zones on her body wept for his touch.

"Smear that oil on you," she instructed.

He glanced down, watching her massage his cock with her foot. "Where?"

"Anywhere you want me to taste you," she replied.

She stopped touching him with her toes, kicking her feet away and sweeping her legs on either side of his, spreading herself to him, knowing her panties wouldn't cover her entirely and the swollen intimate lips hidden in her dark curls would tempt him to obey. A few of Mac's previous fantasies, the ones she'd brought to life by reading his mind, had skirted the edge of domination and submission. The soft leather whip. The velvet handcuffs. The way he loved to take her from behind, taunting her breasts to madness while he pumped into her body. They'd played strangers in the night, even cops and robbers, where the very naughty Lilith had been punished for her crimes in the most delightful ways. But the control had always been his.

Lilith had justified the submissive role by considering it a reversal of type. Her previous lovers had been all too happy to let her take the lead, tell them what she wanted so they could dutifully fulfill her requests. The results had been ultimately…boring.

But not with Mac. With him she'd never asked for anything and yet she'd always been fulfilled by the act of catering to his needs. Sometimes, their sexual preferences overlapped. Other times Lilith pushed herself into positions and situations that blurred her independent streak. She'd become consumed with pleasing him to the point where she'd lost a bit of who she was.

Tonight the breadth of Lilith St. Lyon rose to the surface. Asking Mac to cross the line, to touch himself in that sinfully delicious way, upped the ante between them in ways she'd never imagined. Mac was a man who gave orders. Mac was a man who took what he wanted when he wanted and she'd nurtured that in him by not being who she really was.

But now she had a chance to turn the tables and while his face seemed to have lost a shade of color as he fully realized what she wanted him to do, he straightened his spine and shifted his legs so that his sex jutted hard and hot against his thigh. For the longest of moments Lilith was tempted to eschew her plan in favor of quicker relief for her body's building ache.

To distract herself, she reached between her breasts and unsnapped her bra. "So where do you want my mouth first?"

Mac poured a penny-size amount of oil on his palm.

She eyed his cock. "You're going to need more than that."

He arched a brow. "Am I?"

Dipping his finger in the oil, he smeared his left nipple with the cinnamon delight.

Clearly the man had a glorious way of avoiding her difficult request.

She dropped to her knees in front of him, aware from his hiss when her bra fell aside. She took his nipple into her mouth and suckled long and slow and hard, savoring every spike of cinnamon flavor on her tongue, reveling in the glorious feel of her nipples scraping against his chest. Just as she started to move away, he swirled another dollop of oil on his other nipple. This time she made sure to brush her body across his erection as she moved. Again the exotic zest of the cinnamon exploded on her tongue, but not with the intensity she craved. This time she took the bottle from him and poured a steady stream into his palm, the oil seeping over the sides.

"You know where I want to taste you," she said, leaning her elbows on the couch so her breasts jutted forward.

"I know where I want to put it so I can taste you," he replied.

Leaning in, she lapped up the drops of oil dribbling onto his thigh, keeping her tongue stiff so the sensations burrowed into his skin.

Again she moved back, watching as when he wrapped his hand around his sex and slathered his taut skin with oil. His hands were there and gone much too quickly for her liking.

"I think you missed a spot."

He narrowed his dark gaze. "I did not."

She opened her mouth and slowly rotated her tongue around her lips, emphasizing how she'd soon envelop his cock if he simply did as she asked.

"I say you did," she challenged.

With a quick swipe of her finger she stole a layer of oil off his sex then with painful, deliberate slowness, anointed her dark areola. He reached out to touch her shoulders, but she scooted back.

"Not yet. Not until you get yourself nice and spicy and slick for me. All of you, if you know what I mean."

The way his eyes darkened, she knew he understood completely what she wanted him to do. She had no doubt that Mac had stroked himself to release on more than one occasion in his life—every guy did. Heck, every woman. But obviously, he'd never done so in front of a lover. She wanted him to expose himself in this vulnerable way. By the determined look in his eye, she knew he wasn't afraid.

Just reluctant.

And the reluctant could be swayed.

"You want to see me do this?" he asked, his tone appropriately cocky as he slipped his sex between his greased-up hands.

"Oh, yes," she confessed, snagging her bottom lip between her teeth.

He pulled long, hard and tight.

"Wouldn't you rather do this yourself?" he asked, dipping his hand low on his shaft and again stroking up.

"Oh," she said, her sigh breathy and ripe with wanting as his sex grew visibly harder and tighter beneath his own hands. "Yes."

She made no move to take over the manipulation, and he closed his eyes and continued to stroke.

"What do you see?" she asked, knowing he was visualizing behind his eyelids.

"You," he answered, his rhythm increasing.

Her body throbbed for him. She gasped as a cool bead of moisture seeped from between her legs, kissing her intimately, driving her mad. She grabbed the couch cushions and twisted her hands into the leather, trying to remain still as he pumped harder and faster.

When he groaned, on the brink of release, she couldn't wait any longer. She slapped his hands away and took him fully

into her mouth. The cinnamon flavor was heated, deepened
by the added taste of his arousal, and she suckled until she
heard him cry out her name.

His shoulders drooped and he leaned forward, elbows on
knees, as his body regenerated. She slipped to the side,
moving behind him and smearing more oil over his back,
neck and shoulders.

"I thought I," he said, breathless, "was supposed to
please you."

She licked across his shoulder blade. "You *are* pleasing me."

As she massaged his skin, he hissed when the oil heated
to intolerable levels. Best invention Josie ever stocked in her
shop, Lilith decided. After allowing her to work into his
muscles, Mac spun around, grabbed her and skillfully slid her
onto his lap.

"I want my oil back," he said, prying the bottle from her
slippery fingers.

She didn't fight him. "What are you going to do with it?"

He yanked off the top and drizzled the rest of the oil down
her body, ripping off her panties before they were drenched
in cinnamon-flavored paradise. He trickled a rivulet over each
nipple and then squeezed a concentrated stream directly
between her legs. She gasped, then lost her mind completely
as he laid her onto the couch and proceeded to lave away each
and every drop.

By the time he thrust his tongue inside her, she was mad
with wanting. She tangled her fingers in his hair and urged
him to bring her over the edge with hot demands and lusty
promises. When her orgasm rocked her, she screamed out his
name and for a flash saw him on top of her, thrusting into her,
bringing her complete release yet again.

A split second later, her fantasy came true. He pressed his cock deep within her, filling her to the brink. The combination of flavors and scents and sensations drove them both. Orgasms came hard and fast and without art or gracefulness.

And somewhere in the madness Lilith caught a glimpse of her own future—and this was it.

8

JOSIE STARED AT THE elevator doors. When they closed behind Mac and Lilith, she pressed her lips tightly together.

Now what?

Rick smiled at her, but the grin was nothing short of uncomfortable, which went perfectly with the silence ringing through the deserted lobby.

She didn't have a lot of time to make a decision. She wanted to invite the handsome detective up to her apartment. She wanted to get to know him better. She wanted him to get to know her better. She wanted a date. She wanted a man in her life and in her bed. Not tonight, necessarily, but soon.

She wanted a lot, didn't she?

Well, she wasn't going to get what she wanted without doing something, was she? Look at Lilith. Lord knew the woman had her sights set on Mac again, and despite her rather testy tirade, she'd still managed to ease up to her fourth-floor apartment with the sexy cop in tow. Josie, so far, had done nothing as outrageous as yell at the man she was interested in. Why couldn't she finagle the same result?

"I suppose you have to go back to the precinct now?" she finally said, her voice tremulous. Blessed goddess, why did she have to sound so wimpy? Confidence like Lilith's came from within, and while Josie wasn't exactly brimming with self-assurance, she wasn't exactly a shrinking violet, either. She imagined her friend would have simply crooked her finger and batted her eyelashes until the man fell into a pool of desire at her feet. Except, honestly, Lilith wasn't a bat-the-eyelash type. More a grab-the-lapel-and-take-what-you-want type. There was a life lesson in there, Josie was sure.

Rick glanced at the exit but didn't seem overly anxious to escape. He rocked on his heels and slid his hands into his pockets. "I suppose I should, what with Mac gone."

"Does that put you in charge?"

"Me? Nah. Detective Walters is the senior detective. She's my partner, though, and probably would appreciate the help. Though officially I've been off the clock since we tracked down Mac and Lilith. I worked a late shift last night, then did a second shift when all hell broke loose this morning."

He must be exhausted. She should do the gracious thing and allow the poor man some well-deserved sleep.

"So your partner's a woman?" Josie asked. Okay, first instincts aside, she didn't want Rick to leave. Not yet. And she was genuinely interested in his career. Sharing a cultural background, Josie knew it was no easy feat for a Latino man to take orders from a woman. Or at least that's what she'd been told all her life. She'd only visited her father's new home in Texas a few times, and although she'd found him charming and sweet, her mother had insisted that their relationship had dissolved because he hadn't been raised to handle a free-thinking woman.

She'd always wondered, though. She'd also met her paternal grandmother, and the woman made Susan B. Anthony look like June Cleaver.

"Barbara? She's the best. Top notch. Cool, precise. Knows her shit. Oh, sorry."

Josie smiled. "That's okay. It's nice to hear you so passion-ate about her."

"No, it's not like that," he insisted. "Not that she's not an attractive woman—she is. But I'm like a son to her. Or at least, a younger brother."

Took a few seconds before Josie realized what he meant. "Oh, I didn't mean to imply—oh!" She was such a boob when it came to men! "Let's start again. I'm impressed that you respect your partner so strongly. And, if you're not in a hurry to return to the precinct or go home and catch up on sleep, would you like to come upstairs and, I don't know, grab a cup of tea?" Oh, yeah, that's manly. "Or a soda? I don't have any coffee or beer."

Rick smiled shyly. "Do you have anything with a vintage?"

The twinkle in his deep brown eyes perked Josie's confi-dence. "I do have this bottle a client gave me a few months ago. I have no idea what it is—"

"Sounds delicious."

The pleasured growl in his voice spawned a warmth that spread through Josie's body like wildfire. The elevator seemed incredibly small on the ride up, and though Rick broke the silence by asking her about how long she'd lived in the building, Josie could hardly think for all the tension spiking between them. Could she really be this lucky? A guy like Rick Fernandez interested in her? What were the odds?

She knew Lilith had wanted to warn her earlier. She didn't have to be permanently or temporarily psychic to see the ad-monition in her friend's eyes. But though Josie had experi-enced disappointment after disappointment in the dating department for more years than she cared to count, she couldn't ignore the fact that Rick seemed to stroll into her life at a very opportune moment. *After* she'd had that weird dream last night. *After* she'd had such a strong sense that her life was about to change.

The minute she unlocked her door, Pyewackett, her black-smoke tabby, leaped off the bookcase beside the door and landed directly in their path, hissing loudly.

Rick instantly pushed Josie back against the door. While she enjoyed the sensation of his well-muscled back pressed against her chest, his arms outstretched protectively, she couldn't help but giggle.

"What is that thing?" Rick said, his eyes wide.

"That's my cat," she answered simply.

Pyewackett paced back and forth, his long fur spiked in warning.

"Cats hate me," Rick said, relaxing only a smidgeon.

"Do you hate them back?" she asked. This was a serious question. She'd had Pyewackett for over a decade. She'd known Rick Fernandez for all of an hour.

He dropped his arms and leaned forward slightly, as if attempting to assess his rival more closely. "I have no opinion one way or another. I just know that cats don't warm up to me. Now dogs—dogs I love."

Okay, so she wasn't a big canine fan, but that came from living in small spaces all her life and having no desire to go out in the typically freezing Chicago winter weather to let a dog do his thing when a cat was perfectly content with a litter box stuffed in a nice warm closet.

Shyly she squeezed out from behind where Rick had flattened her.

"Sorry," he said sheepishly. "Reflexes."

She nodded and tried not to lick her lips. "They're very…effective."

Scooping Pyewackett into her arms, Josie decided a little distance might be a good thing. Making a big deal out of cooing to the cat until he calmed, she watched Rick look around her place. This was always a huge test of the men she brought home. Here, in her little corner of the world, she made no secret of who she was and what she believed. An entire curio full of crystals sat beside the aquarium housing the exotic plants she used for potions and the freshwater fish that nurtured them. Her walls, painted a warm cocoa-brown, were filled with photographs of important mystical sites she'd visited. Stonehenge. The Oracle at Delphi in Greece. Tintagel Castle in Cornwall. Chichen Itza in Mexico. Pakaalana Temple in the Waipio Valley on the Big Island of Hawaii.

"Wow," he said, sidestepping her carved coffee table to view the pictures more closely. "Did you take these?"

"Yeah," she said, releasing the breath she'd held tight in her chest. So far, so good. "I used to travel a lot."

"You don't anymore?"

"Business keeps me in one place more than I like, but a girl's got to pay the bills."

He turned, his face perplexed. "I don't think I know what you do."

She laughed as she allowed Pyewackett to drop to the ground. She headed for her tiny kitchen, where she was certain she owned a few wineglasses that weren't ceremonial goblets.

"There's quite a bit you don't know, but we can remedy that as soon as I find some glasses." She ducked under the counter. "I own a shop on Ohio, near the Magnificent Mile."

He whistled. "I'm impressed. That's prime real estate."

"Don't be," she assured him. She made a living, but she was by no means wealthy or in competition with the chichi shops just a block away from her on Chicago's famed Michigan Avenue. "My mother's family has owned the building since the fifties, so I pay no rent. And utilities are negligible except during the winter. The place is mostly apartments, but the ground floor has an Italian restaurant on one side and my shop on the other."

She peeked and found him perusing the books on top of her television. What did she have out again? A Carly Phillips romance. A Stephen King. Maybe her potions book, she couldn't recall.

"What do you sell?"

She found the wineglasses behind the Tupperware and gave them a rinse as she spoke. "Candles, mostly. Custom-made. Aromatherapy supplies. Knickknacks."

Her mention of candles drew him to the shelves where she displayed some of her first creations. She watched him as furtively as possible, drying the glassware more than necessary, but unable to tear her gaze away from his broad frame. He made a beeline for the black candle she'd formed into a cat. Splotched with silver wax and dotted with light green crystals on the face, it looked amazingly like Pyewackett.

"I can see your inspiration for this one," he said, glancing down as the cat stalked him, this time quietly, but with no less potential for danger. Pyewackett had always been incredibly protective of her, which was why she'd chosen him as her familiar.

"He's a good cat, really," Josie assured him. "He just isn't used to strangers."

Rick leaned down and bravely extended his hand as one

would do to a dog. Pyewackett, of course, stared at him as if he'd lost his mind.

"What do you do to warm a cat up?"

Josie shook her head and laughed, her insides effectively melting into admiring goo. At least he was trying. That counted for a lot. "There's no set formula to winning a cat's affections. Just give him time to adjust. Cats are notorious for clinging to people who are uncomfortable around them. You watch. In no time, you won't be able to get rid of him."

From his frown Josie figured that prospect wasn't very appealing. "Need help with the wine?"

Josie had to think about where she'd stashed the bottle. She was by no means a teetotaler, but any wine she normally bought was consumed with Lilith over cheese, crackers and girl talk or alone as she enjoyed a simple, solitary dinner. She didn't entertain much otherwise. She really had to change that.

"If you can find it, I'd be very appreciative," she called out. She checked the top of the refrigerator, underneath her countertop and in the back of the pantry. She was about to give up and offer Rick a lemonade when he came into her four-by-four kitchen with the bottle of Shiraz clutched in his hands.

"It was on your chest of drawers."

Chest of drawers?

"Where? I don't have…"

Oh, yeah. She'd used the wine to represent the earth portion of the four elements on her altar. She'd set it right next to the vial of water, the wand carved from birch for the air and the candle she'd dipped in various shades of purple and blue for fire. Her chest tightened as she realized how exposed she was. What did he think? Did he care? Did he simply not notice?

He turned to point out where he'd found the bottle when Josie grabbed his face impulsively and kissed him. She wasn't sure if she'd been possessed more by the need to keep him from realizing that her "chest of drawers" was actually a Wiccan altar or by her insatiable desire to experience his smooth lips on hers. After a few seconds, her motives didn't matter.

Sensations riding on a wave of hot, vibrating tingles assaulted her from all directions. She speared her fingers into his hair, and seconds later his body, tensed at first by surprise, relaxed and molded into hers. She heard the clunking of glass on countertop as he deposited the bottle, and in the next movement his arms were around her.

His hands were strong, splayed on her hips like possessive bands. His tongue softly slipped into her mouth, coaxing her to moan as the sensations built in her body. Her nipples tightened and she knew he could feel the hardness through her loose blouse. When his sex pressed against her belly, she jolted. Was this too fast? Too forward?

Too exciting for words?

Gently he eased back, breaking their intense connection, though desire darkened his eyes to pitch black.

"Wow," he said.

"Yeah," she agreed, her fingers dancing lightly over her swelled lips.

"I seem to say that word a lot around you."

She blinked in surprise. "Why?"

He shook his head and turned toward the wine, busying himself with unraveling the foil wrapping on the cork. "You're different."

Funny, but that sure didn't sound like a heart-stopping compliment. "Am I supposed to say thank you?"

"I mean you're unique. Really different, in a good way, from the women I usually date."

She narrowed her eyes, waiting for the punch line.

"Because I'm, what, more like the women you arrest?"

He didn't answer, but the way his lips tightened testified that he wanted to say yes. She grabbed the drawer pull and yanked, fishing for the corkscrew she knew she owned. Suddenly she had a very powerful thirst for alcoholic beverages.

She found the opener and used all her self control not to stab him in the palm when she handed it to him.

"I didn't mean to imply—"

"No, I'm sure you didn't," she said sweetly. "Most men don't get lucky by comparing the women they are with to prostitutes and scam artists."

She nearly choked on the last two words, blocked by the hypocrisy of her righteous indignation. Wasn't as though she hadn't lived that life in her youth, scamming people out of their hard-earned cash and keeping one step ahead of the law. But she'd been a kid then, doing what she'd been told, what she'd been taught from birth. Still, guilt was a hard and heavy cloak to remove, especially when the world could be so cold.

He put the bottle down and moved to take her hand. She slipped past him, but he followed.

"Josie, that's not what I was implying at all. Look, I spend nearly half my day with my partner, who is good for a laugh but for the most part she's all business. That's what it takes for a woman to make it in a cop's world. When I go home to Miami, my mother fixes me up with women who are sweet and funny and…average. Nice, but without spark. I mean, what mother wants her son to find a woman who sparks?"

She spun toward him. "What about here in Chicago? What kind of woman turns you on here?"

"The kind who talks too much when she's nervous. The kind who cares about her friends enough to walk into a bar on the South Side without even a bottle of pepper spray. The kind who invites a charming cop to her apartment and offers him wine she can't even find. The kind who grabs a man by the face and kisses him soundly just because."

Josie pursed her lips. Oh, man. He was good. *Charming* didn't even begin to describe. Hot. Sexy. Undeniably sexy. So sexy she could feel a trickle of moisture curling between her thighs, readying her body for sex in ways she hadn't experienced in a long time.

She fought to look him in the eye. "I had pepper spray," she admitted.

He grinned, his straight white teeth dazzling against his dark skin. "Resourceful, too. See? Different. Surprising. Spontaneous."

Unable to stop herself, she glanced down. His crotch was showing all the obvious signs of arousal and while the idea that she'd inspired his physical reaction turned her on even more, she wasn't about to screw this up by jumping too hard and too fast.

"Not too spontaneous," she warned.

He took a step back, his hands raised in mock surrender. "Message received. Now how about that wine?"

LILITH ROLLED OVER, HER muscles aching in the most amazing ways. Maybe it wasn't so bad, not having her psychic powers. Without her ability to read minds, she'd been totally surprised by Mac's willingness to play love slave for hours on end. He'd been entirely devoted to ensuring her pleasure and while she'd never gone unsatisfied when she had used her abilities to become his dream woman, she couldn't deny a deep fulfillment from turning the tables. Maybe there were advantages to not knowing exactly what a man wanted or planned to do to you before he did it.

Maybe? Who was she kidding? There were *definite* advantages.

Slithering through the sheets, she was only half surprised to find his side of the bed empty. She listened for the shower but, hearing nothing, peeked one eye open. He'd pulled the shades so the room swam with sleepy shadows instead of bright morning light. Damn, the man was a keeper.

Too bad she couldn't keep him. It was one thing for him to accept that she, just days ago, had possessed the power to read minds and have insight into the future. It was something else entirely for him to accept her entrenchment in a world peopled with witches and hunters and the occasional demon. Mac was an amazing man, but he was a man. He had his limits.

Limits she'd think about later. After they had morning sex. "Mac?"

He didn't answer. Not wanting to sound like a harpy, she rolled out of bed. As she stood, the full force of the bourbon hit her. Not a slam, really. She hadn't drunk that much. And, besides, she was no stranger to hangovers. More like a slap she could soothe with a splash of cold water and a couple of painkillers. She brushed her teeth, ran damp fingers through her hair, then wrapped herself in a filmy robe she had hanging on the back of the door.

She found Mac on the far side of the living room, his head

pressed against the window as he whispered into his cell phone. She went into the kitchen and noisily made tea. By the time the whistle sounded on her kettle, he'd finished his phone call and was standing in the doorway, looking entirely delicious in nothing but his boxer shorts.

"Sleep well?" she asked.

"Will you be offended if I say no?"

She grabbed two mugs from the cabinet. "Offended? No, but I might be challenged to work you a little harder next time."

Provided there was a next time.

"Promises, promises," he said with a grin.

She pressed her lips together and busied herself with trying to fish Earl Grey tea bags out of her varied collection. Without coffee, strong black tea was the best she could do. She poured the water and set the bags to brew.

"So what's your plan for today?"

He ran his left hand through his hair. He still clutched his cell phone in his right. "For the first time since I can remember, I have no plans at all."

After squeezing the tea bags and tossing them in the sink, Lilith plopped a cube of unrefined sugar into each mug and handed him the steaming drink, which he eyed warily. "It's tea."

"I figured," he said, taking a tentative sip.

"What did I serve you in the mornings…before?"

He frowned. "I don't think I normally hung around. Remember, back then I had a job."

She led him into the living room. While she grabbed her favorite throw blanket and curled up on the couch—a normal morning activity for her—he paced. He put the phone on a table, paced, then picked it up again.

"I have ideas about what you can do with all that pent-up energy, you know."

He smiled, but the grin was forced. She didn't take it personally. Mac Mancusi was not a man of leisure. He needed a project. A purpose. And unfortunately for her, teaching him to paint her toenails or even enlisting him to help her hang the prints she'd bought from Josie's store weren't going to fill his increasingly empty well. Mac needed a challenge. A cop challenge.

"Who was that on the phone?" she asked, taking a sip.

"Fernandez," he answered.

She arched a brow. "He wasn't at Josie's, was he?"

Mac sat down beside her on the couch, cradling the mug between his hands—hands that could be ravenous or gentle, depending on his intentions. "I didn't ask."

She waved her hand at him. "You men are no fun. Aren't you curious if they hooked up?"

"No," he answered.

"Don't you like Josie?"

Mac nodded. "I like her a lot. That's why I'm not curious. Let her live her own mistakes, Lilith."

"So you think her hooking up with Rick would be a mistake, too?"

He shook his head before taking a long sip of the hot tea. "I'm not having this conversation with you."

Lilith consoled herself with her tea for a few moments, then scooted closer to Mac on the couch. "Okay, we won't discuss Josie's love life. What about telling me what Rick *did* discuss on the phone? And before you tell me you can't repeat what he said because it's department business, let me remind you that you are no longer, albeit temporarily, part of the department."

Mac blew out a frustrated breath as he leaned back on the couch. "They found Pogo Goins's car burning in an abandoned lot in Cicero. It had been stripped, doused with gas and torched to a crisp. Word is also out that the street-level dealers are out of sight right now, which probably means they're picking up their goods and getting ready to distribute."

"Can't your undercover DEA agents get a bead on the location of the pickup point?"

He arched an eyebrow.

"Hey, I listen when I'm at the precinct."

He arched the other eyebrow.

"Okay," she conceded. "I watch cop shows on television, too."

"You know too much."

"Too much to be dangerous," she verified.

"I don't want to drag you into anything dangerous."

"Too late. Not only is sleeping with you incredibly risky, but you asked me to help you with the Goins case. That's all I'm doing."

"This is bigger than Goins now. He's dead."

Lilith nearly dropped her cup. "How? In the car?"

Mac shook his head. "Bar owner found his body in the alley this morning, and the coroner's not sure about cause of death. There were no visible signs of upper-body trauma. No knife wounds. No bullet holes. No strangulation marks. Just weird scorch marks on his shirt. No real damage to the skin underneath."

This time the cup went tumbling. Tea splashed her legs and doused Mac, as well. He jumped up and cursed, but Lilith remained still, trying to regulate her breathing.

Scorch marks?

"What the hell?" Mac's voice rose.

Lilith started to shake. She took in several deep gulps of air, hoping she'd heard wrong. Scorch marks on clothing that did no visible damage to skin, but caused death were the signs of only one kind of weapon she knew—energy bursts. Like the kind Regina wielded as Guardian. The ultimate defensive weapon against magical creatures who sought to destroy the witching world.

They weren't used on mundanes. No one—not good or evil—wanted to open that can of worms.

"Lilith, what's wrong? You look like you've seen a ghost."

She shook her head vehemently. Oh, no. No ghosts. Ghosts tended to spook the shit out of her, but they couldn't do damage in the corporeal world. But Mac didn't know that, did he? Even she didn't think about such matters most of the time. Most witches didn't. They lived in the mundane world the same as everyone else, existing and thriving, living and loving, with only rare encounters with the truly unexplained.

"His skin wasn't burned?" she finally managed.

"The initial ME observation guesses a lightning strike or some sort of electrocution, but noted that there didn't seem to be a visible entry or exit wound for the juice. They're stumped. There will be a full autopsy, but no one's sure when since the initial finding is classified as accidental death."

Suddenly conscious of her surroundings, Lilith whipped off the throw blanket and started to sop up the spilled tea. Though her instincts screamed death by energy burst, she simply had to be wrong. Goins wasn't mixed up in the magical world. He was a low-level drug user who'd simply been in the wrong place at the wrong time. Or was there more…?

"Who called in the report?"

Mac leaned forward on his elbows, watching her intently. "Business owner. Lilith, what do you know? Are you having one of your premonitions or something? 'Cause I'm sure Rick can sneak us into the coroner's office if that'll help you get a hint of who killed Pogo."

Lilith shouted in frustration, a primal growl that spawned from the deepest part of her soul. Uninhibited, she leaped to her feet, stamping her bare flesh against the hardwood floor, trying to grab onto what had been so unfairly taken from her. She was so helpless without her powers. And if she called Regina again, what would she be proving to the Council? That her big sister had to ride to her rescue or intervene in her affairs in order for her to be truly helpful to others?

And what if there was some other explanation for Goins's injury? She couldn't risk exposing her world, not if she ever wanted back in.

She had to try and figure this out on her own first.

And to do that, she had to lie. Or at least be slightly misleading.

"I'm not sure," she said. "But I think maybe a trip to the coroner might be a good idea."

Mac jumped up like a child who'd just been given a free pass to Disney World. He dialed Rick's number and moments later had formulated a plan to sneak Lilith in just after noon, when the coroner went to lunch.

"How many laws are we breaking?" Lilith asked, wondering if bending mundane rules would be looked down upon by the Council, and, frankly, wondering why the hell she cared.

Mac shook his head. "I won't go in with you. You've worked with the police department on cases in the past, so technically no laws will be broken by letting you in again. But if you had your powers stripped—whatever that means—how can you be getting vibes now?"

Lilith slid her mug onto the table, staring into the remnants of the now barely warm liquid, wishing that reading tea leaves was a real magical art and not simply a visual representation for psychics who truly had the gift—and a lot of shysters who didn't. She was on her own here, torn between doing the one thing she'd never really done to Mac before—told him a lie—and 'fessing up to a very hard-to-believe truth. She had always kept the secrets of the very real, very powerful magical realm. She'd had no choice. All witches, upon receiving knowledge and training with their powers, pledged silence for the safety of their community. They could break the vow, but only under extreme circumstances. And while Pogo's mode of death might qualify, she had to examine the body first to be sure.

"Mac," she said finally, acting on the fear of losing the tentative connection they'd reestablished, "I can't explain why I have to look at Goins and I'm not sure that doing so will help anything. But there's no harm in trying, right?"

Mac's eyes narrowed. "There's something you're not telling me."

She took a deep breath. "Yes, there is."

He glanced aside, his expression tentative when he faced her again. "But you want me to trust you on this, don't you?"

A glob of something thick and hot formed in the back of her throat. How could this man, with no magical powers, understand her so well?

"For now," she managed to choke out. "I don't want to lie to you. Ever."

He leaned forward and swiped a soft kiss across her cheek. "Then for now that's all I need to hear."

9

LILITH WAS NOW CERTAIN that she never, ever wanted to be a cop. Fernandez quietly slid the metal drawer back in place, then gestured her out of the freezing-cold morgue. Josie had given her a small bundle of lavender and chamomile to hold to her nose during the viewing of Goins's body, and while the simple herbs had offset the rank medicinal smells, they hadn't blocked the shock of witnessing the evidence of a mundane killed by a magical energy burst.

"Anything?" Fernandez asked once they were in the hall.

Lilith shook her head. Without her powers, she'd received no insight into Goins's death, no flash of his final moment, no image of the killer. Of course, she didn't have to be psychic to know that even men like him who rode roughshod over lawfulness weren't ordinarily killed by energy bursts. The skill to wield something of such lethal power was reserved to a select few. Upper-level demons—and there weren't many of those left. High witches who acted as Guardians or members of the elite protection squads oftentimes controlled the power, but none but a rogue would use it against a mundane. She considered the possibility of a warlock who'd stolen the power from someone else, but warlock activity was monitored by the Council. If a warlock was running loose in Chicago, someone would know. Wouldn't they?

Lilith had no clue as to who had murdered Pogo Goins—but she did know that the magical realm had intersected with the mundane world in a way that was not good.

Mac met them at the car. He talked quietly with Fernandez while Lilith slid into the passenger seat, wrapping herself tightly in her hand-woven sweater despite the heat, in no mood to drive. She didn't find her voice until she and Mac were on the road, headed to her apartment.

"So it was a bust?" he asked.

She gasped, thinking for a moment he'd said *burst* instead of *bust*.

"I told you it probably would be," she said quickly, covering her reaction. "But I had to try." Even if she really hadn't. What was the point? Her powers were gone. She'd only agreed to view the body to verify that the death had indeed been caused by a magical burst of energy.

It had.

Which meant some magical being existed in Chicago who could block said existence from Regina and the Council.

Someone powerful.

Sly.

Cocky.

Like…Boothe Thompson?

The idea snuck into Lilith's brain quietly, then exploded in a wild blast of supposition. Could this be why she could never read the wily attorney? Why he seemed to track her down at the precinct and at the bar with so little effort? Warlocks keyed in on a witch's magic with the same stubborn skill as a police bloodhound. But why then hadn't he attacked her? Warlocks and witches made lions and zebras look like bosom buddies.

Unless he didn't need her power.

Or he didn't want to bring down the wrath of the Guardian by attacking her sister.

Or maybe he was biding his time, specifically to lure Regina into danger.

Lilith dropped her head into her hands. Too many theories with no proof gave her a massive headache.

Mac reached over and slid his hand gently across her knee. "I'm sorry for putting you through a morgue visit only to come up empty. You probably don't like be reminded of what you've lost."

Her jaw dropped open, but she squeezed her lips tight before he noticed. Thoughts of Boothe Thompson flew out of her head, thanks to Mac's insightful comments.

"Same goes for you," she replied.

He nodded knowingly.

Lilith adjusted the air conditioner, suddenly warmer. "Fernandez leak you any new information?"

Mac shook his head. "Nothing except that Boothe Thompson identified the body. Goins's girlfriend was called, but it was Thompson who showed up."

Lilith turned and faced Mac squarely. "Why him?"

"No one knows. The girlfriend came a few minutes after Thompson left—and she wasn't happy. Clearly, she didn't like her man's mouthpiece very much."

"If she didn't call him to ID the body, how'd he know about the death? Did someone in the department tip him off? Would someone in the department tip him off?"

The Mustang's engine roared as Mac shifted into a higher gear. "No clue, but I intend to find out."

With one determined phrase, Mac knocked the malaise

right out of Lilith's body. Nothing stoked Mac more—well, almost nothing—than having a defined purpose. Before, Lilith had considered his devotion to his job charming but a little stereotypical. Robotic, as if he worked his job simply because that's what the men in his family did, from his great-great-grandfather in Italy to his father here in Chicago. She didn't realize till right this moment how they both came from families with deep tradition to service. Difference was, Mac took his obligations seriously. Lilith, on the other hand, spent too much time lamenting how her power wasn't as strong or as important as her sister's. She supposed she hadn't truly understood what it meant to have a calling until she lost hers.

"What does your brother do?" she asked.

"Excuse me?" Mac asked, not following the sudden turn in the conversation.

"You have a brother, right? But he's not a cop?"

Mac snorted at the possibility. "No, Derek is a professor at the University of Illinois, Chicago."

"Criminology?"

"American literature, particularly the Romantic period. Something incredibly impressive yet embarrassing at the same time."

Lilith, warmed by the admiration in Mac's voice, lowered the fan on the car's AC. "He doesn't regret not going into law enforcement?"

"Nah. Once I followed Pop's footsteps, I cleared the way for him to do whatever he wanted. No pressure for him."

"Real or imagined," she added.

"What?"

"Never mind," she said, not quite ready to share what she'd learned about Mac and his brother and how it paralleled her and Regina. The conclusions would not put her in a very good light.

Lilith had spent too much time comparing herself to Regina. She'd tried to convince herself that she'd never wanted the responsibility Regina's position entailed, but without her powers, her emotions had moved out of the way and she saw the truth with the clarity she should have possessed with her clairvoyance. Her sister hardly lived in the real world at all, bound to the Registry in Sedona and to the Council. She had little time to kick back, relax, have fun. Dabble in romance. The one time Regina had shirked her responsibilities and let loose to pursue a man, she'd nearly paid with her life.

Lilith, on the other hand, had all the freedom she could handle and more. She lived among mundanes and made a decent living off predicting their futures. Sure, every once in a while she'd help Mac solve a crime or find a missing person or assist in an interrogation, but mostly Lilith lived for herself.

Now, when she truly wanted to help Mac and the city avert a drug-related crisis, she had nothing to offer except the suspicion that someone from her world with the power to produce deadly energy bursts was behind the whole mess. Someone who might be hidden right out in the open.

"Fernandez is risking a lot feeding you information," she said.

"Rick's a good cop," Mac said, emphasizing the word *good* as if a cop's worth was measured more by his commitment to justice than his adherence to the dictates of the mayor. "Detective Walters is acting chief detective, and apparently she was told, in no uncertain terms, to stay away from Goins and Thompson."

"Even now that Goins is dead?"

Mac clucked his tongue. "Goins was a known drug user. The evidence on the body points toward an accidental death."

Lilith chuckled humorlessly. "A lightning strike in the middle of a Chicago alleyway on a clear day?"

"Electrocution of some sort."

"Did your colleagues find any wires or open circuits anywhere near his body?"

Mac frowned. "No, but it did look like the body had been thrown quite a distance."

Lilith nodded. She'd seen Regina send a practice dummy flying at least fifty feet. "But I'm betting there weren't any live wires anywhere, were there?"

He slowed at a stop sign and looked at her pointedly. "Could have been a jacked-up Taser."

"With no marks on the body?"

"Do you know something you're not telling me?"

She chewed on her bottom lip and wondered how much, if anything, to say to Mac. Somehow she couldn't see him accepting the truth. Not without proof. Convincing him she was a genuine psychic had required nothing less than him writing and hiding four messages in various spots around her apartment, then watching her find each and every one and reciting the contents of the envelopes without unsealing them. It had started out as a game.

Sure as hell hadn't ended that way.

But short of conjuring her sister and asking her to demonstrate how energy bursts worked—something she was one hundred percent certain Regina would refuse to do—she decided that avoidance was the best tactic.

"I have some ideas, but I want to do a little research. We can't go chasing wild theories, now can we?"

"I have nothing better to do."

"You could go home and change clothes," she offered. While she couldn't care less that Mac was still wearing the same shirt and pants from yesterday, she needed an excuse for a little time alone. She had a theory—one she could only explore without Mac peeking over her shoulder.

He sniffed his sleeve. "Yeah, I guess I'm ripening as we speak."

She leaned across the seat and buried her nose into his arm, inhaling deeply. His cologne had long burned off his skin, but the sensual scent of musk and man nearly made her dizzy with need. Her nipples hardened beneath her blouse and her skin prickled with the thought of him skimming his rough fingertips across her naked flesh. "Just thinking about you taking a long, hot shower gives me all sorts of wicked ideas."

"Then come with me," he invited, his voice husky. "Two people in my shower is a bit tight, but I'm sure we can survive the squeeze."

Oh, the temptation. But she needed to scare up a laptop since hers had been returned to the manufacturer with a faulty motherboard. Josie had one, but she'd need the computer after the store closed to work on receipts and inventory, so Lilith would have to get it now while the store was still open. Besides, she and Mac could use time apart. Lilith needed space to decide how and when—and if—she was going to reveal her entire self to a man who would certainly run the other way once he knew the whole truth.

Oh, wouldn't the Council be *thrilled* about that.

"You make an irresistible offer," she admitted, curling back into her own seat.

"And yet you're going to resist," he concluded.

"Just until later. I have some stuff to do."

Mac watched Lilith's eyes and knew from the quick dart of her gaze that she wasn't being entirely honest. Maybe she just needed a little space. Last night had been damn intense, and the renewal of their affair after their horrible breakup had come out of left field. Come to think of it, he could use a dose of distance himself.

"Want me to drop you off at your place?" he asked.

"No, at Josie's store. She has something I need."

Mac complied. When he eased his Mustang to the curb beside The Crafty Cat, which he assumed was some kind of knitting or craft-supply joint, Lilith surprised him by leaning across the seat and dropping a soft kiss on his lips before departing. The act, so natural that she barely seemed to notice she'd done it, was incredibly intimate. Funny how making love to her six ways from Sunday paled when compared to a simple gesture that promised nothing…and everything.

Mac pulled back into traffic, his heart suddenly pounding hard in his chest. He skirted the speed limit, moving in the opposite direction as quickly as possible. Instead of heading for his apartment, he found himself on the highway and, soon after, in front of his mother and father's house in Tri-Taylor. He parked on the street and slipped through the wrought-iron gate that was never locked. Everyone in the neighborhood knew that a retired Chicago police detective lived there and that Angelo Mancusi wouldn't hesitate to shoot any intruders first and ask questions sometime after he finished a celebratory can of Old Style beer.

Despite his mother's admonitions to walk in whenever, he knocked before using his key.

"Anyone home?"

"In here," his father answered.

As expected, he found his pop in the den, reading glasses perched halfway down his nose, a pile of receipts stacked on the worn and battered desk he'd taken home from the police department on the day he retired. It had been a big joke. Never once in a twenty-year career had Angelo Mancusi ever been relegated to a "desk job." He'd never once been suspended or even put on administrative leave for firing his weapons—something they didn't do automatically in the old days. Angelo had been a cop on the street, mixing it up, bringing in informants and cracking cases other detectives had abandoned as cold and lost causes. Mac had had a hell of a time fitting in Angelo's shoes. Frankly, despite his promotion to chief, he still didn't consider himself half the cop his father had been.

Now he'd been suspended. Why he'd come here of all places, he hadn't a damn clue.

"What's going on?" Mac asked, listening for his mother, who didn't seem to be puttering around anywhere close by.

"Your mother's at her cooking class," Angelo informed, holding a collection of receipts like playing cards and reading his son's mind thanks to familiarity and not any supernatural skill.

"Mom's taking a cooking class?" he asked, incredulous.

His father guffawed. "Taking? Teaching! Down at the university. Your brother got her to volunteer. Apparently the coeds in his class got tired of hearing how delicious his mother's cooking was. She's teaching the girls how to make real spaghetti sauce and meatballs with a hot plate. Craziness how women don't know how to cook anymore."

Mac wondered if Lilith knew how to cook. He'd never

seen her do more than brew tea or pull munchies out of the fridge, but that didn't mean much. She could be a gourmet chef, for all he knew.

His father took off his glasses and stared at him pointedly. "What are you doing home in the middle of the day?"

Mac shoved his hands in his pockets. "Thought I'd drop by Al's for an Italian beef and wondered if you wanted to come along."

Angelo considered his son carefully. Mac employed every last ounce of his self-control not to shrink under his father's assessing gaze.

"Yeah," he said, placing the paperwork in a neat pile before struggling to his feet. "Your mother made me minestrone for lunch. Meatless. I could use something a little more substantial."

Despite the shuffle in his father's sixty-nine-year-old gait, Mac complied with Angelo's request that they walk the six or so blocks to Chicago's famous Little Italy eatery. The more they moved, the spryer Angelo became. By the time they reached Al's—impossible to miss with its bright red illuminated awnings—he was walking like a fifty-year-old.

"Don't tell your mother I came down for a beefsteak. She'll drag me back to that doctor to check my cholesterol again."

"How's that going?" Mac asked.

His father snarled. "I'll tell you all about it after you tell me what the hell happened at the precinct yesterday."

Mac held the door open for his dad, shaking his head and chuckling. "How'd you find out?"

Angelo stared at him incredulously. "You don't think something like the Chicago chief of detectives getting canned makes the evening news?"

"I wasn't canned," Mac corrected. "I was suspended."

His father arched a brow. In the end, vocabulary choice made no difference.

"I can only thank St. Anthony that your mother went to bed early," his father continued. "I swiped the paper, too—told her the Gallianos' dog peed on it. If someone doesn't ask her about it at the university, you can tell her yourself when we get back."

Mac hadn't considered…damn, he'd been distracted. First by Lilith, then by Boothe Thompson, then by Lilith again. Not that he was complaining. Obsessing over news reports of his suspension and hearing the inevitable misinformation would only have aggravated him to the point of insanity. He'd been much better off playing love slave to Lilith's sensual mistress of the night.

"Sorry, Pop. I didn't think the mayor would let the incident hit the news. He was all hot to keep the situation on the down low."

"The mayor," Angelo said with disdain, "If his last name ain't Daley, he's no mayor of mine."

"What did the article say?" Mac asked, only half of him wanting an answer.

"Just that you had a disagreement with the mayor about procedure and had opted to take a two-week suspension rather than make a big deal out of it. But that's not true, is it?"

Mac didn't bother trying to lie to his father. He'd tried and failed often enough as a teenager to know the exercise was fruitless. "No, Pop. That's not what happened at all."

His father silenced him with a hand as they blended into line to order four of Chicago's finest Italian beef sandwiches, two for each of them. Over rolls piled with paper-thin slices of seasoned meat and hot giardiniera relish, they waxed hopeful about the Cubs' next season, switching to the Bears as they headed over to Mario's for Italian frozen lemonades.

"So what really happened?" Angelo finally asked as they pounded the pavement back toward the house.

Mac retold the story, leaving out nothing, including following Boothe Thompson to the dive bar and Pogo Goins ending up dead shortly thereafter, his car found but destroyed. Okay, he left out the night of hot sex with Lilith. Some things you simply did not share with your father.

"And this woman, this psychic," Angelo asked, not sounding as doubtful about Lilith's abilities as Mac would have expected, "she couldn't see anything about the murder?"

"You believe in that stuff, Pop?"

Angelo laughed heartily, the mirth causing a belch he didn't bother to cover. "When I was a cop, we'd take all the help we could get, even from the crackpots who begged for dimes on the street corners, because crackpots have eyes like everyone else. You don't get to my age without seeing and hearing a few things that don't make sense. Doesn't mean I'd fall for any scam artist in a tea shop, but some of these people are real. Ask your mother. Her grandmother had 'the Sight.'"

"What?" Mac asked. His great-grandparents had been born, lived and died in Sicily. They'd been strict Catholics who'd eschewed all things paranormal as evil and wrong. Hadn't they? Come to think of it, Mac wasn't even sure he knew the first names of his great-grandparents, especially on his mother's side. And he'd certainly never heard any stories about grandmothers with precognitive abilities.

"Back then, it was no big deal," Angelo assured him. "Every village in Sicily had an old woman, maybe more than one, who could predict the future or maybe cast a curse or two. The evil eye, they called it. Wasn't just Gypsies who could work that magic. Why are you getting all uptight?"

"I'm not uptight," Mac insisted.

"Then why does your jaw look like its going to crack?"

Angelo didn't beat around the bush. Mac exercised his jaw until he felt the joints and tendons relax. "I just never heard that about Mom's grandmother before or figured you to buy into that mumbo jumbo so easily."

Angelo shrugged, unrepentant. "You get to my age first and then you tell me what's real and what's not. Until then, I'm just stating facts. Some people know stuff before it happens. Some people can tell you stuff after it happened, people who weren't even there. I had a case once where this crazy woman called the precinct every day telling me that Joan of Arc came to her in the shower to tell her where to find a missing load of cash from a bank heist. This woman was an invalid and had no ties to the bank robbers, who we'd caught and had in custody. Damn it if Joan of Arc wasn't right about the location. We recovered every last penny. After that, I was willing to follow any lead no matter how ridiculous. Especially if the psychic isn't hard to look at," he said with a smile.

Mac frowned in response. "I didn't say anything about what Lilith looked like."

"You didn't have to. I could hear your dick hardening in your voice."

Mac stuttered, trying to come up with something to offset his father's sudden crudity.

"Hey, the stork didn't deliver you to my front yard, boy. And I wasn't born yesterday."

Mac decided the best course of action was to turn the conversation away from his physical reactions to Lilith and back to the case that had so far resulted in him being suspended, the death of a potential informant, the impending release of a huge drug shipment onto the streets of Chicago and a reunion with the woman he'd never thought he'd see again, much less sleep with. Much less care about. A lot. More than he wanted to. More than he should.

"The last time we talked about sex, Pop, I was sixteen. And I mean the *last* time."

Angelo found Mac's discomfort hilarious, laughing loudly enough to draw his mother to the front door.

"I thought that was your junk heap parked by my begonias!" she shouted from behind the screen. "I suppose you two went to Al's before you bought those gelatos."

"It's not gelato, it's ice. Fat-free," Angelo said, offering up his foam cup.

Viviana Mancusi threw up her hands with a demonstrative "Bah," then disappeared into the house, muttering about throwing out the fish she'd prepared for dinner since Angelo had clearly already had his fill of tastier food.

He shrugged. "She worries about my eating habits."

"You think she shouldn't?" Mac said, eyeing his father's protruding belly.

Angelo patted the paunch with pride. "I married her for her looks, so can I help it if she's also great in the kitchen?"

They slipped into the den while Mac's mother continued to bang pots around in the kitchen. Mac made a note to butter her up extra when he went in to say goodbye. Angelo wrapped up his bill-paying project by shoving the receipts in a shoe box and turning back to his son, this time his expression dire.

"So tell me about this murder in the alley."

Mac recited the scant evidence the department had collected.

"For someone on suspension, you sure know a lot."

"My suspension is strictly a political move, Pop. All the

guys in the department know that. They aren't going to shut me out because I lost my temper with an attorney they all hate."

"Good for them," Angelo declared. "And this psychic couldn't read anything when she saw the body?"

"She says no," Mac replied.

This caused Angelo to arch his bushy eyebrows. "You don't believe her? Is there more to this story than you're telling me?"

"Loads," Mac replied.

"Then it's personal."

"Too personal."

The cacophony coming from the kitchen stopped, followed by a burst of music with the volume turned up high. Dean Martin. "Ain't That a Kick in the Head." Both men winced. When Mac's mom started playing Dino, she was seriously pissed off.

"You think she's angrier about the cholesterol or the fact that you had a snack and ruined dinner?" Mac asked.

"How do you know she's not ticked off at you for not giving her a kiss when you saw her at the door?"

Pop had a point. There were rules to be followed around this house, and in keeping with his new, Lilith-inspired attitude to eschew popular canon and make his own way in the world, Mac had made a serious Mancusi-house faux pas.

"I'll go in first," Mac said, heading toward the kitchen.

"Brave man," his father responded.

They chuckled down the hall, but before Mac turned the corner, his father tapped him on the shoulder. His expression was half serious and half not, so Mac had no idea how to prepare for what was coming next.

"You be careful with that psychic lady, okay? You never know what you might find out."

"About the Goins murder?" Mac asked.

Angelo cursed in Italian, then gave Mac a playful slap on the cheek. "No, *mi figlio,* about yourself."

10

LILITH HAD FOUND HERSELF at the train station without a single memory of walking the four blocks it took to get there from Josie's shop where she'd picked up her friend's laptop. She boarded the red line, transferred to the blue and disembarked along with a cache of UIC students into the old Little Italy area. She wasn't sure why she'd gravitated here, but she didn't question her instincts, especially now that she knew exactly where she was headed.

A long walk across campus later, she opened the door to her favorite Taylor Street hangout. The tinkle of the bell over the doorway provided an instantaneous prelude to the incredibly decadent scents that assailed her. Cinnamon and cloves. Sugar and yeast. Butter. Lots and lots of butter. Lilith could have floated into Natale's Bakery on the cloud of temptation rising in the long-established Italian confectionery's ovens, but she walked instead, her mind already working out which delicious treat she wanted.

The selection was impressive, even after the lunch crowd had long gone. Lilith had frequented the bakery enough to know that they'd close in less than two hours and that the smells emanating from the back were to fulfill the late-afternoon restaurant orders. Fortunately, Lilith spotted a lone cannoli in the case, and her mouth watered in anticipation of the sweet cream filling and crunchy pistachio surprises.

When no one emerged from the back, Lilith leaned across the counter and spotted Izzie—the owner's daughter who seemed to run the place single-handedly lately—lingering near the hallway to the office.

"Izzie?"

The curvaceous, olive-skinned former dancer yelped in surprise. "I'm sorry," she apologized, wiping her hands on her apron and hurrying over. "My head was in the clouds."

"If the clouds all smell like this bakery, that's not a bad place to be."

Izzie shook her head, her ponytail swiping against her shoulders. "Believe me, it's not so great going home from work with hair scented like anisette and clothes that reek of ginger."

"On the positive side, they say the scent of licorice is great for dieters because it controls your appetite," Lilith mentioned, though, looking over the baker's killer body, only barely disguised beneath the apron, she didn't think Izzie had a thing to worry about.

"Twizzlers can have at it. I try to ignore the smells unless someone burns something."

"Oh, come on," Lilith teased, a little surprised by the usually cheerful Izzie's pessimism. "No one at Natale's ever burns anything."

Izzie rolled her eyes and gave her hands a quick wash in the sink before opening the back of the bakery case to pull out Lilith's selection. Scooping up the cannoli with a piece of thin, crackly paper, Izzie started to reach for a take-out bag.

"Do you mind if I hang out a while?"

Changing directions, the young woman placed the cannoli on a milky-green china plate. "Got a reading?"

If only. Lilith ran her hands through her hair, tugging a little harder than necessary on the strands. "Nah, I'm taking a break from the medium world right now."

Izzie sighed. "Just my luck. For the first time in my life I think I'd actually *pay* to have someone tell me who the heck I'm going to be next week."

Lilith shrugged the laptop strap more securely. "Honey, so would I. My so-called vacation from clairvoyance isn't by choice. But if you hand me that cannoli and whip me up a cappuccino, as soon as I'm back on the job, you'll be the first person I work with."

Izzie scrunched her nose but handed her the plate. "Might be too late by then," she lamented.

Lilith blew out a frustrated breath. "For the both of us, friend, for the both of us."

She took a table by the window while the cappuccino machine whooshed and burbled and coughed up pure caffeinated heaven under Izzie's skilled hand. By the time she had the computer up and running and hooked into the free Wi-Fi Natale's offered their café customers, Izzie came over with a steaming ceramic mug brimming with the milk and espresso, blended with two sugars and dusted with cinnamon exactly the way she liked it.

Lilith took a sip before clicking onto the Internet.

"Doing some surfing?" Izzie asked.

Lilith dug a fingerful of sweetened ricotta cheese out of an open end of her cannoli and hummed her appreciation of the delicious filling as it smoothed over her tongue. "I'm going to try. The most I've ever used the Web for is updating my Web site and answering e-mail."

"Don't forget shopping," Izzie suggested, a joke in her tone. "Or maybe you're going to start haunting chat rooms?"

Lilith blanched. "No. I'm doing…research."

"Oh," Izzie said knowingly, as if she had any inkling of what Lilith was about to undertake. Lilith wasn't exactly sure if the mundane Internet could help her prove her theory—that Boothe Thompson was a warlock. But until she was prepared to summon Regina or the Council decided to restore her psychic abilities, this was all she had.

"Let me know if you need anything else," Izzie said before strolling back behind the counter and losing herself, once again, in deep thought and pastry.

Lilith bit her bottom lip, hating the wash of helplessness splashing over her. She used to give Izzie little tips from time to time, most of which the headstrong young woman ignored. While Izzie and most of the regulars at Natale's knew Lilith worked as a psychic reader, no one, save her clients, really believed in Lilith's clairvoyance. So few people did, which was how she managed to stay under the radar. She was a well-liked curiosity, mostly because she gave her predictions as if they were simply strong opinions from a mouthy psychic who wore funky jewelry and sexy clothes.

Lilith hadn't really cared how the mundanes saw her or what they thought about her as long as they paid for her readings in cash. She'd never gotten excited over her predictions being correct because, well, of course they were. She wasn't making educated guesses. She'd been plugging into a power that was as old as time itself. She'd been taking her gift for granted, she now realized. She medicated the empty feeling that realization caused by taking a huge bite of cannoli.

Lilith wasn't the most computer-savvy person in the world,

but she did know how to Google. She found the search engine and typed in Boothe Thompson's name.

She read article after article about the wily attorney, including a bio that claimed he was from a small town in upstate New York she'd never heard of. Ditto the law school. Funny. She'd expected Harvard or Yale. With nothing of note in the Web section, she clicked the link to Google Images and started again.

She got a chill from every single snapshot. Boothe Thompson smiling with the mayor on election night. Boothe Thompson addressing a crowd of reporters outside a high-profile trial he'd just won. Boothe Thompson curling his arm around a beautiful blonde with vacant eyes at some charity function. Willing the Italian pastry she'd eaten not to explode right out of her stomach every time she caught sight of Thompson's oily, practiced grin, she clicked and clicked and clicked until she found a picture that might serve her purpose.

She enlarged the photograph and squinted at the laptop's fifteen-inch screen. In this picture, his hand was definitely visible. Flush against his tuxedo jacket at some charity soiree, his left hand glittering with his signature ring. Something about the jewelry had caught her attention back at the precinct, but she'd been too distracted to look closely. Now her instincts screamed for her to revisit his jewelry. Because warlocks were known show-offs, the ring might be her only clue to proving her theory.

She needed to see the ring close up, but she couldn't chance meeting with Thompson again until she knew what she was up against. If he was a warlock, he might kill her, as warlocks preferred to do to witches. He couldn't, at least, execute his main purpose—stealing her powers. That had already been done, though chances were he wasn't aware of that little fact.

If she met him, it would have to be in public.

But first she had to be sure that he was what she suspected. She needed to enlarge the photograph, focus on the ring the way they can do on the cop shows on television.

But how?

"Hey, Izzie," Lilith called just as the door opened and the bell jangled. "What do you know about computers?"

Izzie greeted the new customer, a leggy brunette dressed entirely in sleek black leather. Lilith glanced out the window and caught sight of a Ducati motorcycle. She liked this chick already.

"Well, I don't know how to find any naked pictures of Heath Ledger and I haven't figured out how to send a death ray to spammers, but I do the Web site for the bakery," Izzie offered.

Lilith watched the newcomer lower her sunglasses to eye the café menu, then turned her attention back to Izzie.

"So you know how to enlarge pictures? Other than ones of naked movie stars?"

Izzie grinned. "Yeah, give me a sec."

The new patron and Izzie chatted while Lilith tried to be patient. She drank more of her cappuccino and finished her cannoli in two bites. She wondered about where Mac was right now, then, gazing out the window at the sandwich shop and lemonade stand across the street, remembered that he'd grown up only a few blocks from here. Was that why she'd gravitated toward this side of town today? Or had her craving for decadent Italian sweets been purely accidental?

She didn't believe in coincidences. Nothing happened without a reason.

"So what do you need?"

Lilith jumped at Izzie's sudden appearance, but this time

laughed in response. Eventually she'd get used to not having her extrasensory perception. Or, better yet, she'd get her powers back and would look back at this time as a bitter memory. Except for Mac. She'd remember him with bone-melting pleasure, that was for sure.

"I need a close-up of this guy's ring."

Izzie leaned toward the laptop and squinted. "It's pretty big already."

"Not big enough."

Izzie sat down and slid the laptop toward her. Her fingers flew over the keys and type pad with confident ease, but when she turned the screen back toward Lilith, the picture was all distorted.

"That won't work," she said.

Izzie shrugged. "You need a higher-resolution picture."

Lilith grunted. She vaguely knew what that meant. More pixels per square inch or something. She flipped back to the Google Images page, but while this picture appeared several times, none offered the resolution she needed.

"How can I get a higher-resolution picture?"

"Where'd you get the first one?"

This from the stranger in black, who hovered a few feet away, her hands wrapped around a steaming mug.

Lilith would take any help she could get. "Newspaper Web site."

"They'd use a lower resolution there so the page will load faster. They'd probably only use high res in the actual printing process."

Lilith frowned. "I don't have any contacts at the paper. I don't think they'd give access to their archives to just anyone."

The stranger arched a brow, a tiny grin quirking her full, generous lips. "Do you want access?"

Oh, Lilith really liked this chick a lot. She didn't have to have her powers to read the edgy wickedness in this woman's posture, expression and smile.

"Most definitely."

The brunette put her coffee down and threaded her fingers together to give them a stretch. Lilith scooted the laptop around to give her room to work, but she simply leaned over the machine and worked standing up, her eyes darting periodically outside the plate-glass window of Natale's.

"Nice ride," Lilith commented about the Ducati.

Her fingers didn't slow. "Gets me around. Who is this guy, anyway? Don't tell me you're trying to figure out if that ring is a wedding band and he's the asshole you've been dating for the last two years."

Lilith nearly spit out the last of her cappuccino. "Ew."

The stranger nodded in approval. "So he's not your lover."

"Say that again and I'll dump the dregs on you. He's a jerk I'm investigating."

"A jerk?" The stranger snorted. "What makes him different from every other man on this planet?"

"Good question," Izzie muttered. With no other customers in the shop and closing time quickly approaching, she'd begun wiping down tables. Lilith silently hoped the stranger would hurry. She needed to return the laptop to Josie, but more than that, she needed to know if Boothe Thompson was a minion of evil as she suspected.

"Name one guy who isn't a complete asshole," the stranger said, swiping her tongue over her shapely lips as her concentration deepened.

"Mac Mancusi," Lilith whispered.

"You know Mac?" Izzie asked, surprised.

Damn, Izzie had good ears.

"Biblically," she replied.

Izzie's eyebrows shot up. "No kidding? You and Mac? Wow. I can't picture the two of you together."

Who could? "You won't need to. We won't be together much longer."

"You're dumping him?" Izzie asked, clearly disappointed. "You're right, you know—Mac's not a jerk. He grew up just a few blocks from here. Our families know each other. I'd think any woman would love to catch a good, honest cop like him."

The stranger stopped her work. "You're sleeping with a cop."

Lilith pushed the laptop closer to get her to resume what she suspected was illegal hacking. Goddess bless her.

"I'm sleeping with him, I'm not married to him," Lilith insisted. "Trust me when I say that my definition of right and wrong varies from his by huge degrees. Keep working and your next ten espressos are on me."

The stranger smiled and returned to her task. "I won't be around that long, but thanks for the offer."

"Add her to my tab," Lilith instructed Izzie. "Anytime she stops in, coffee's on me. What's your name?"

"Seline."

"Does that mean you're actually going to pay your tab someday?" Izzie asked, an amused grin tugging at her full lips. Her mood had apparently improved.

"Soon. I swear."

Lilith tapped her fingers impatiently on the table, stopping when Seline gave her a warning glare. This woman's computer savvy could result, ultimately, in the returning of Lilith's powers. Only then could she get her income going again so she could actually pay bills like her bakery tab.

The longer Seline worked, the deeper she frowned, her dark gaze glued to the screen, her hips swaying back and forth as if the rocking motion enhanced her ability to think. "Don't get ahead of yourself. I haven't got it…wait…ding, ding, ding. We have a winner."

Lilith clapped enthusiastically. "I had a feeling you were up to the task."

"You would," Izzie quipped.

Not only had Seline found the picture in a higher resolution, she'd enlarged the picture so that Boothe Thompson's hand filled the entire screen. At first glance, Lilith had to use all of her self-control not to throw back her chair and chant the incantation to summon Regina immediately.

It was there. The red sickle symbol of the warlocks, embedded in the stone.

Instead she took a deep breath, blew it out slowly and willed herself to remain calm.

Seline eyed her suspiciously. "Is that what you need?"

Lilith saved the image to an e-mail addressed to herself and backed it up to Josie's hard drive, then shut off the machine and tucked it in the bag. "Unfortunately, yes." She stood and extended her hand to Seline, who, after a moment's hesitation, gave it a strong shake. "Thanks for your help. If you ever have need of a psychic, look me up. Well, in a few weeks, when I'm back on the job." She patted the laptop case. "I think I just found my golden ticket back to gainful employment. Izzie, thanks for the sugar boost and the Wi-Fi."

Izzie waved. "Anytime."

Lilith weaved through the tables and chairs until she reached the door. The bell had just jangled when Izzie called out, "Lilith!"

Lilith turned.

"Don't be so quick to write off a great guy like Mac," Izzie said, her voice tentative, as if she couldn't quite believe she was offering romantic advice. "Maybe you and he can find a way to make it work, even if you think there's no way it ever could."

She gifted her favorite baker with a smile, but didn't respond. How could she? Now that Lilith had this information about Boothe, she could make huge inroads with the Council. Chances were, she'd have her powers restored very soon. And when that happened, she doubted Mac would stick around. They'd made this little reunion work because she hadn't been able to freak him out with her mind reading. Once she regained her powers, she couldn't see how two such divergent people could make a relationship work.

She waved to Seline and started back up the street to the university, where she'd catch the train back to the city. After a few blocks, she had her concentration fully on what she'd discovered. She didn't give Mac and his soft touch and warm tongue and intelligent humor a second thought.

Well, not a third thought, at the very least.

Boothe Thompson wore a warlock's ring. Boothe Thompson knew that Pogo Goins had nearly slipped up and revealed potentially damaging information to the police. Boothe Thompson, darling of the Chicago social set, had a predilection toward representing crime bosses and low-life criminals like drug dealers and thugs. Warlocks often gravitated toward the dregs of mundane society. Made them feel superior. A ring was not proof that the lawyer was a warlock, nor that he possessed the power to form and launch energy bursts, but the evidence was clearly pointing in that direction.

And if so, she had to figure out how to stop him. If, as she suspected, he'd murdered Pogo Goins and left his body to be discovered by mundane cops, the attorney wasn't afraid of exposing the magical world. Of course, warlocks were essentially nonmagical and relied only on the powers they could siphon from witches or demons. They didn't care too much about making messes.

And somehow this particular warlock was operating under the radar. Normally, a protection squad directed by the Guardian or the Council would have disposed of Goins's body before his mysterious murder could be discovered, and the warlock would have been promptly dispatched to the lower realm. Why hadn't that happened?

Lilith needed to contact Regina, but fear held her back from ducking into an alley and saying the summoning spell. A witch like Regina would be an incredible catch for any warlock. With Regina's enormous powers at his disposal, a warlock could change the balance between good and evil for centuries. And with Regina still recovering from her last battle with one of the magical world's big bads, could she win?

Maybe Lilith could handle this herself. As a mundane. In public. If he couldn't steal her powers, Thompson wouldn't risk exposing himself by hurting her so long as she didn't come across as a threat. A little subtle finessing and she might find out first if Boothe Thompson was indeed a warlock and second if his supernatural status had any connection to the crime wave rocking Chicago. If, in the process, she figured out who was behind Mac's big drug shipment, wouldn't that rock?

She was just about to cross the street when a familiar rusted Mustang pulled up in front of her, the passenger-side window rolled down.

"I could have mowed you down and you wouldn't have noticed me honking," Mac groused.

Lilith looked behind her, noticing for the first time how far she'd walked without being aware of her surroundings. She was nearly past the university. "What are you doing here?"

He leaned across the seat and opened the door. "I was about to ask you the same thing."

She slid into the car. "I craved cannoli. Sue me."

He chuckled. "Get any for me?"

She shook her head. "I got Izzie's last one, sorry."

Thankfully the conversation turned away from their odd and apparently coincidental—ha!—meeting while Mac drove her back to the city. She told him about having to return Josie's laptop before her friend closed the shop, so he braved the gridlock on Michigan Avenue and delivered her with fifteen minutes to spare. A car pulled out of a metered space and Mac slid in with precision.

Lilith opened the door but hesitated before going in.

"Wait for me?" she asked.

His smile was sly and sensual. "Absolutely."

11

JOSIE GLANCED AT THE clock hanging above the row of dried herbs and flowers, then stared at the glass door leading to the outside. Reminding herself that a watched cauldron never boiled, she busied herself with rearranging the pomegranate candles she'd put on the counter in anticipation of the secret society convention happening at McCormick Place this week. She'd imbued the bloodred candles with a variety of essential oils and herbs beyond the base of fruit pulp and pure beeswax. She'd blessed the candles for riches. For power. The usual for the secret-society types. She'd also included a few drops of a special blend meant to enhance clarity and encourage the discovery of true love. To balance the greed for world domination.

Even though the convention didn't start for a few days, the candles had already sold like hotcakes—with each and every conventioneer paying in cash. She couldn't help but smile ruefully at how people tried to hide what they were. Ben Franklin might not have been Wiccan, but he showed his timeless wisdom by saying, "three can keep a secret when two of them are dead."

The thought led her back to Lilith. After the lunch-break crowd had thinned and Lilith had come in begging to use her laptop, Josie had whipped up an extra batch of the secret-society candles, intending to give a few to her friend. She'd also taken one candle for her own personal use, convinced that if she and Rick were going to move past the shy-flirtation stage they'd started yesterday, they were going to need some intervention from outside forces.

When the crystals hanging above her door jangled, Josie was not surprised—though not entirely excited—to see Lilith rushing in instead of Rick, who was due in forty-five minutes.

"I'm so sorry!" Lilith said, breathless. "I nearly missed closing. You're going to have to recharge the battery, I think."

Josie held up the power cord already plugged into the surge protector on her counter beside the antique cash register. "Ready to go. Did you find what you needed?"

Lilith laid the computer case down gently on the counter. "Yeah," she said with a grunt.

Josie unzipped the case, removed the laptop and connected it into the charger. "You don't sound excited about it."

Lilith pressed her lips tightly together, a telltale sign that her friend wanted to confide in her, but was holding back. Josie busied herself with booting up the computer, wondering where on Earth everyone got the impression that she was made of glass and couldn't handle being saddled with problems, big and small. Lilith. Her mother.

Lilith and she had been friends for five years. She was privy to just about every secret shame Josie possessed, including her arrest record and her less-than-idyllic childhood. More importantly, her mother had lived the craziness with her and had witnessed firsthand how Josie had pulled herself out of insanity and built a thriving business in one of the toughest, most competitive shopping districts in the United States. Blessed

Hecate, but her mother had been the reason behind most of the troubles she'd faced and survived—why couldn't she at least acknowledge her inherent strength?

Josie took a deep breath. She'd hoped the aftereffects of her mother's phone call two hours ago would have worn off by now.

They hadn't.

"Are you going to tell me what you found out?" she asked, emboldened by her ire.

"I want to," Lilith said reluctantly.

"Then tell me. Is it about Mac?"

Lilith shook her head. "It's about Boothe Thompson."

"The attorney you chased down last night? Ooh," Josie said, her ears perking at the idea that Lilith had dug up something juicy—something that would take her mind off her own life for a bit. She hadn't been around the defense attorney for long, but the man's aura had screamed smarmy. Creepy, even. "Is he a cross-dressing Liza Minelli impersonator in his off hours?"

Lilith burst out with laughter and they both dissolved into giggles at the visualization of the slick, high-priced lawyer in Broadway-bound drag. After a minute, Lilith wiped a tear from beneath her eyelash and pulled in a deep breath. "Thanks for that mental picture. I'm going to hold on to it for future reference. But, no, that's not what I found out."

"Okay, the well-respected lawyer isn't a secret drag queen," she said, groaning with disappointment. "What is he that has you so troubled?"

Lilith took another deep breath, then expelled her words in one quick rush.

"He's a warlock."

Josie grabbed the edge of the counter, her heart stopping short. "A—"

"Warlock. And I'm not talking Samantha's father, Maurice, either."

Josie shook her head emphatically. No, she'd never even considered the dapper tuxedo-wearing character from the television show *Bewitched* a real warlock, no matter what they called him on the show. On the contrary, warlocks were just below demons as the vilest creatures in witch lore— emphasis on the word *lore*. As in, not real.

As in, the stuff of nightmares. The stars of stories children told each other at sleepovers.

"What makes you think he's a—?" She could barely say the word, not when Lilith clearly believed the creatures to be real.

Lilith turned the laptop around to face her, clicked a few keys, then opened up the photograph of a man's hand—more specifically his ring.

"See that symbol?"

Josie stared at the quarter-moon shape intently, knowing she'd seen the exact image before somewhere else. Not something recent. A book. She dashed to the private, off-limits library she kept behind a curtain in her office. Fishing the key out from the necklace she wore beneath her blouse, she unlocked the bookcase and scanned the aged and withered spines for the tome she sought.

"Here," she said, yanking out a blackened leather diary. Lilith had followed her. Josie spread the book onto her desk, the musty scent of old paper assailing her. "I've seen the image before."

She paged through the volume, flying past the fading ink drawings and journal entries from a practicing witch who had lived in Mexico over a generation ago.

"What is this?" Lilith asked.

"Book of Shadows."

"Yours?"

Josie laughed. "Hardly. I keep mine digitally."

"In your computer?" Lilith asked, sounding half impressed and half shocked. Every practicing witch was encouraged to keep a Book of Shadows, to record her spells, potions and ritual traditions. Through the books, other witches could follow the customs of their ancestors. Most of the books were incredibly routine and, to a long-practicing witch such as herself, a little boring. But every once in a while Josie stumbled upon a book that testified to potions, rituals and spells that were amazing in their results. Powerful. Instantaneous. Magical, in the truest sense of the word.

She kept the books guarded and hidden, safe from falling into the wrong hands.

"I used to save it on a disk drive until the flash drive was invented." She fished the tiny computer device out from another chain she wore around her neck. "I never leave home without—"

A drawing deep in the book stopped her short. A blood-red sickle carved into the arm of a man whose eyes reflected pure, unadulterated jealousy and hate. Beneath the drawing, the word *Warlock* curved in bold calligraphic text.

"That's it," Lilith said. "That's the exact symbol I saw the night my mother—"

"These are real?" Josie asked Lilith, tapping the picture with her fingernail, unable and unwilling to hide the fear in her voice.

Lilith nodded.

"How can you be sure? Have you ever seen one?"

The breath escaped Lilith's lips on shaking waves. "Briefly. When I was little."

"How do you know it was a real warlock? I mean, little children make up all sorts of bogeymen. Warlocks don't exist. They're fairy-tale creatures that are sometimes part of the mythology of our craft."

"That's what the Council wants witches like you to believe."

"Witches like me?" Josie asked, not wanting to feel offended...but feeling so anyway. Something in Lilith's expression reflected...superiority. "As opposed to witches like you?"

Lilith took the book and scanned the entry, clearly oblivious to the condescension in her last comment. "Where did you find this book? The Registry should have this. It shouldn't be just floating around."

The Registry? "In a shop in Sedona," Josie answered, crossing her arms on her chest. Lilith had been a good friend to her, but sensitive of other people's feelings she was not. To their thoughts, yes, but their emotional state often escaped her notice. Being self-absorbed wasn't a crime in Josie's eyes—but prejudice was. How exactly did she and Lilith differ as Wiccans? From what Josie had observed, she practiced more regularly and with more reverence than Lilith ever did.

"Answer my question," Josie insisted. "How are we different as witches?"

"Sedona?" Lilith asked, sounding surprised and still not answering her question.

"Yeah, Sedona. What's so surprising about that?"

The artists' colony in Arizona was widely renowned as an epicenter for paranormal and spiritual pursuits.

"Josie," Lilith said, then her face altered. She reached out and grabbed her hands, squeezing tightly. "Oh, that didn't come out right. The 'witches like you' thing. That's not what I meant."

Josie wasn't done nursing her annoyance. "Then what did you mean?"

Still holding tight to Josie, Lilith pulled her to the nearby settee. She sat beside her, but her eyes were focused on the ceiling, as if she'd somehow receive guidance from the heavens. The idea of Lilith asking anyone for help beyond borrowing a laptop or a pocketful of dried herbs seemed utterly ridiculous.

"I shouldn't tell you too much," Lilith said. "Not because I don't want to but because it's sort of against…well, it isn't a good idea. In a nutshell, there are two separate levels of witchcraft. You practice Wicca and follow the creeds and codes of the craft. Yours is a long tradition of people who have followed the ways of the goddess."

"You're Wiccan, too," Josie pointed out.

"Yes," Lilith agreed, but her tone implied there were extenuating circumstances. "My family is Wiccan, but even if we weren't, we'd still be witches. We belong to a second level of witches. A line that dates back to the roots of our beliefs. A collection of witches with…active powers."

Josie sat back against the stiff, needlepoint cushions, wondering if along with her ability to read minds, Lilith had lost her marbles. "You mean like on *Charmed?*"

"*Charmed* was a vast exaggeration of our world."

"But based on truth?"

Reluctantly Lilith nodded. "To a degree. The media has portrayed witches incorrectly from as far back as *Bell, Book and Candle* to *Harry Potter* and *Charmed.* No one has portrayed us exactly as we are—and, to be honest, we're okay with that. I've always suspected the misinformation was done on purpose. The more our world is accepted only within the realm of fiction, the safer we are from mundane concerns."

Josie's eyes felt as if they had started to spin in their sockets. She closed them tight and tried to concentrate on all the craziness coming out of Lilith's mouth.

Craziness that might not be crazy at all.

"Mundane?" she asked.

Lilith blew out a shaky breath. "I know that sounds like I mean boring, but I don't. That's the word we use for people who have no active powers or those non-Wiccan."

In the pit of her stomach Josie felt a burble of absurdity. She pressed her hand tight to her abs, trying to trap the laughter in her belly. She was certain if so much as a chuckle popped out of her mouth, she'd sound madder than a hatter. "You mean like muggles," she said, borrowing the term from J.K. Rowling.

"Sort of, yes."

Josie nodded and for a split second wondered if Lilith truly had stepped over the edge. However, Lilith had made a factual connection between the symbol embedded in Boothe Thompson's ring and an ancient marking in a book Josie was quite certain Lilith had never seen. And her friend, while non-conformist and rebellious, had never once shown signs of mental incapacity.

Better to listen. Hear what she had to say. "What do warlocks do in this other level of witchcraft world you're talking about?"

Lilith grabbed the book off the desk and laid it in Josie's lap. "They kill witches and steal their powers. A warlock is ordinarily a male child of an upper level female witch and a mundane male, albeit one with a nasty soul. Evil, but without magic. You know, murderers, serial rapists, etc. The male child will inherit no magic from his mother, but at puberty he will develop an insatiable hunger for power. The only way they can feed their need is to steal magic from another upper-level witch. A warlock's first kill is usually its mother. These aren't creatures that should be dealt with by out-of-work psychics and craft shop owners who only now learned they exist."

Finally, Josie felt the gap between her and Lilith squeeze tight. But if Lilith were really telling the truth, what else existed in the world that she had no idea about?

Upper-level witches? Warlocks? Were demons real, too?

"This sounds like a very dangerous discovery," Josie said, rubbing her arms to dispel the chills raking over her skin. "Who does one report warlocks to?"

"Usually my sister."

"Regina?"

Josie had met Lilith's sister, and while she found the striking brunette an utter contrast with her seriousness to Lilith's devil-may-care personality, she'd never sensed anything in her that pegged her as a witch. In fact, she'd always wondered if Regina practiced the craft at all, despite knowing that Lilith's family had been Wiccan for generations.

"She holds a position called Guardian. She has…means at her disposal to fight warlocks."

Josie ran her hands through her hair, hoping the information would sink in. "Then why didn't you tell her instead of me?"

Lilith leaned forward, burying her face in her hands. "Because those means make her a very valuable catch for a warlock. If Boothe Thompson is what I think he is, he can't steal anything from me since my powers have been stripped. But he could kill Regina—and trust me when I say that the magic she has at her disposal is not something you want a warlock to possess." Lilith took a deep breath. "And I can't call her until I'm sure I can't handle this myself. What if I'm wrong? What if she attacks Boothe and he's just some jerk with a stolen ring? I have to be sure."

Josie glanced around her office, eyeing all the Wicca-related items she'd collected over the years. Some she meant to sell. Some she'd kept for her own. None had ever made her suspicious that a world existed within this one, a world peopled with witches who could spew magic from their fingertips.

Josie was a strong woman. But a strong witch? She might have thought so ten minutes ago, but not now.

"Have you told Mac at least?"

"I can't."

"Why not?"

"I shouldn't even tell you," Lilith replied.

"Are you going to get in trouble?"

"No more than I'm already in," she said with a snort. "There's no witch law against revealing yourself to a fellow Wiccan, but it's certainly frowned upon. There's an element of danger I've just introduced into your life, isn't there?"

Josie winced. "I suppose. But I'm your friend. I'm honored you told me. I'm shocked that I'm believing you, but I am. Trouble is, I can't do anything to help. Mac's another story."

"Telling a mundane cop? The risks are incalculable."

Josie supposed Lilith knew more about this than she did, but the knowledge Josie lacked in regard to sacred witches, warlocks and demons, she made up for with an innate sense that Mac was not only a good man, but a reliable one. "He may not be supernatural, but he's a great cop, Lilith. He cares about you. He'll protect you if he can."

Lilith straightened and jammed her fingers hard through her spiky dark hair. "He'll never believe me."

From the doorway the sound of a man clearing his throat rumbled.

Mac stood, his mouth tight with what Josie guessed was either anger or mistrust or both.

"Try me."

LILITH EYED JOSIE LONG enough for her friend to get the hint.

"Oh!" Josie said, jumping to her feet. "Why don't I go get my work done in the other room while you two…talk. Take as much time as you…"

Mac stepped fully into the office, allowing Josie to tug out the pocket door that separated the two rooms. Mac crossed his arms, bulking his chest in the most delicious of ways. Lilith tried to keep her mind on important things like the potential presence of a warlock in Chicago, but damn if lusting after Mac wasn't a much more interesting path for her brain to take. Rather than, oh, telling him stuff about her life that would make him run—fast—in the opposite direction.

"Got tired of waiting?" she asked, attempting to inject cheerfulness into her voice.

"Something like that," he replied.

Clearly she wasn't pulling off the innocent act.

She got up off the couch and smoothed her moist hands on her jeans. "Let's head back to my place," she suggested.

He planted his feet even with his broad shoulders, making it clear he wasn't going anywhere.

"Okay, let's stay here, then. Josie has a great collection. I'm sure she wouldn't mind staying open late if you want to buy me something."

"Lilith," he said, her name a clear warning.

She groaned in surrender. "How much did you hear?"

"Of what you said to Josie? Only that I wouldn't believe you. Lilith, if there is one lesson I learned from our breakup it was that when you say something, you're telling the truth—at least partially. You tried over and over to convince me that your powers of perception were real. My mistake was that I never really believed you until that night."

Lilith matched his protective stance with one of her own. "Well, then let me be *completely* honest. I didn't try *that* hard to convince you or I would have. Sure, I told you, but a short demonstration would have gone a long way."

"Then why didn't you?"

"Because you would have freaked out. Because you would have hightailed it out of my life quicker than I could say *hocus-pocus.* Don't deny it, because that's exactly what happened."

He stepped closer and the air between them charged. In a split second, Lilith relived the ugly scene of Mac's first departure. And from the dark shadows in his irises she could tell, Mac was experiencing the same loud and nasty rerun.

"I thought we were past this," he said softly.

"We are," she conceded. "But just because we've forgiven each other doesn't mean the memories don't hurt, that we both haven't learned valuable lessons from that horrible night."

Mac closed the distance between them. His scent teased her, making her dizzy with need. "Yes, I learned that I had the capacity to throw away the most interesting, most beautiful, sexiest woman I've ever had in my life simply because I couldn't expand my limited worldview."

She quirked an eyebrow, wondering at Mac's sudden self-awareness.

"Limited worldview?"

"I had a lot of time to think today," he explained.

"I didn't leave you in the car that long," she quipped.

A chuckle broke the electric tension spiking between them. "I'm talking about the entire day, Lilith. From the moment I woke up in your bed until I walked into this shop and heard you doubt me, I've done nothing but think about what you mean to my life. I also spent some time with my father. He gave me some food for thought about accepting who you are—and that means all of you. The world you live in, the challenges you face. The secrets you keep. Particularly the secrets you keep."

Lilith fell into Mac, overwhelmed by his words and knowing, because he was Mac Mancusi, man of honor, he meant what he said.

At least he'd mean it until she revealed her secret.

Blessed be, but she wanted to unload her suspicions. More than anything, she wanted to hear him say that they could face any danger together, even a threat spawned in a world he never imagined existed and likely could never accept. But Mac was a mundane. A man. He'd have no weapon that could fight a creature like a warlock, especially one who could wield an energy burst. He'd need magic to fend off an attack—the one thing she did not have to give. And she couldn't draw him back into her life just to lose him again…maybe permanently.

The image of Mac lying on a slab in the morgue, electrocuted like Pogo Goins, jumped into her brain. She tensed, thinking she'd experienced a premonition—then realizing she'd only had a vision of her greatest fear.

She pulled away from him, wandering back to the settee, where the Book of Shadows sat open to the page about warlocks. Absently she bent down and flipped it closed. She couldn't give him what he wanted. Not now. Perhaps not ever.

"I'm sorry, Mac. I can't unload this on you now."

"If not now, then when?" he asked, his volume amplifying along with his anger. "I can't wait forever."

"We just reconnected yesterday," she reminded him. "You can't expect me to trust you again so soon after what happened between us."

As planned, her words hit their target hard. Mac took one step back, then two.

"What happened three months ago?" he asked. "Or last night?"

Before she could say anything, he was out the door. She heard Josie say something to Mac. He responded curtly, but Josie's volume rose with her insistence. Then there was only the wild tangle of sound from Josie's wind chimes and then nothing.

Josie darted into the office, her face pale. "You told him?"

Lilith shook her head, clutching the Book of Shadows to her chest. "I couldn't."

"Why not? Lilith, did you see the look on his face? You might never get him back now. Not after all you two have been through. How could you not trust him?"

Though she could feel her heart ripping in two deep within her chest, Lilith fought and won against the splash of tears threatening to spill from her eyes. "This isn't about trust."

"Then what is it about?"

Lilith tore toward the door herself, but stopped, not wanting to run into Mac if he was still outside. She opted for the back door leading to the alley. Josie grabbed her arm as she passed.

"What is it, Lilith?"

"Warlocks aren't to be messed with, Josie. It's bad enough I told you. I wish I hadn't. But I have to check this out further and I can't put you or Mac in danger. I have to do this on my own."

She tried to pull out of Josie's hold, but for a petite little thing, the girl had a grip. With a pointed glare, she instructed Lilith to stay still. She went into the workshop beside her office and returned with a small cardboard box. She took the Book of Shadows away from Lilith, shoved the box into her arms and then slammed the book on top.

"What's all this?"

"The box is candles. Light them. The book I'm letting you borrow simply to read about what you're supposed to do. I'll let you out of here if you promise me you'll either consult your sister or Mac before you get anywhere near Boothe Thompson."

Laden with Josie's gifts, Lilith was in no position to argue.

"You know," Lilith said, a smile teasing the corners of her mouth, "you can be really bossy when you want to be."

Josie didn't smile back. "I'm worried about you."

A chill shot through Lilith's bloodstream. Josie wasn't the only one who was worried. She needed time to think. The minute the Council had stripped her of her powers, her world had spun so that she didn't know which way was up. As much as she wanted to protect Regina and Mac, she wasn't a fool. She'd lost the gift she'd relied on her entire life to guide her. She needed her clairvoyance back more than anything, but short of that, she needed to think long and hard before she acted.

Lilith stretched over the box and kissed Josie on the cheek. "Don't worry. Have you ever known me to do anything stupid?"

Josie glanced through the doorway where Mac had just exited.

"Just once," Josie replied, then tapped the top of the box. "But if you're as smart as I think you are, you'll fix it."

12

BLINDED BY FURY, MAC tore onto the sidewalk and slammed into...someone, nearly dropping the candle Josie had forced into his hand before he left. He spun, furious that someone dared crash into his hasty exit, when Rick Fernandez held up his hands in supplication.

"Whoa, there. I'd hate to add assaulting a fellow officer to your list of troubles."

Mac took a deep breath, shoving air out through his mouth instead of the string of curses stomping on his tongue. "Sorry," he muttered.

"Where are you going in such a hurry?"

"The hell away from here. If you were smart, you'd turn tail now while you still have a chance."

Rick glanced past Mac at the door to Josie's shop. From the glimmer in the guy's eye, Mac knew Rick wasn't going anywhere without the owner. Mac wondered if he knew what Josie's store really sold, but he figured his pal would find out soon enough.

"Doing some shopping?" Rick asked, eyeing the thick candle.

Mac smirked. He hadn't wanted the thing, but Josie had insisted, and while he'd been ready to bite someone's head off, Josie didn't deserve his rudeness. There was a jaded innocence about the woman that Mac liked. Josie was cool. Her best friend, however, was a different story altogether.

"Gift from your girlfriend," Mac explained. "Says it's supposed to calm my nerves and give me clarity."

Rick's expression changed from expectant to wary. "A candle can do all that?"

Mac shrugged. "I'm willing to stand on my head wearing nothing but a smile if it'll give me a lead on the drug shipment. Any more word on what specifically killed Goins?"

Rick's lips curled downward slightly. "Backlog at the morgue. Should get to the autopsy by tomorrow."

"Keep me posted?"

"You know it. Look, gotta run. I'm taking Josie to Navy Pier."

Even Mac's foul mood couldn't keep him from cracking a smile. "Isn't that sweet? Gonna propose on the top of the Ferris wheel?"

"Hey," Rick reacted, his words sounding not entirely convincing. "I only met her yesterday."

Mac remembered what had happened between him and Lilith less than twenty-four hours after their first meeting. Wasn't exactly a marriage proposal, but they'd been practicing for the honeymoon like felons who'd had no conjugal visits while in the slammer.

"Yeah, well, take it slow anyway," Mac advised. "Josie's cool, but she's…different. Know what you're getting into before you jump the gun."

Rick rolled his shoulders as if itching for a fight, but his expression remained relaxed. The man was experiencing a serious case of the hots. If not for his natural tan, Mac might have suspected he was blushing.

"Thanks, Pop. I'll take it under advisement."

Which meant the minute he crossed the threshold into Josie's shop, Mac's warning would fly right out of his head.

Probably a smart move. Who the hell was he to dole out relationship advice? He couldn't even convince the woman he'd made love to the night before that he was worthy of her trust. Well, he was sick of her secrets. Sick of her truths that weren't really truths at all.

Mac drove back to his apartment, the candle from Josie on the seat beside him. He nearly left it behind, but didn't want to deal with melted candle wax embedded in his leather seats. After parking, he grabbed the fragrant gift, shaking his head all the way to his apartment. There weren't enough scents or herbs or whatever the hell she mixed into her custom candles to undo the torment raging through him. What he needed was a hot shower and a good belt of bourbon. Or six.

An hour later, neither the scalding water nor the smooth heat of booze had lessened his aggravation. Lilith had been on the brink of telling him something huge. He'd seen it in her eyes, in her body language. But she'd held back, chosen not to trust him. So maybe he had broken more than her heart when he'd reacted so badly all those months ago. He'd thought they'd moved beyond that.

He'd apologized. They'd worked together to track Boothe Thompson to the dive bar where Pogo Goins later died. They'd made love in ways he'd never imagined. He'd taken the role of her love slave, damn it. Didn't she see how hard that had been for him?

He lifted the bourbon bottle to his lips, but didn't drink.

Becoming her love slave actually hadn't been hard at all.

With a growl, he screwed the cap back on the bourbon and

tossed the bottle onto a nearby chair. Jamming his hands through his hair, he tapped down the urge to scream in frustration. He cared about Lilith, but he had no clue what she wanted from him. Beyond sex. Beyond trust. He'd given her both and he had nothing to show for it but a big fat candle sitting in the center of his coffee table, taunting him with the promise of relief.

He had nothing to lose. In the kitchen he found a box of matches. In the living room he lit Josie's candle and waited for the flame to lick at the wax at the base of the wick. The minute the fire kissed the blood-red candle, interesting scents filled the air.

He leaned back into the cushions and closed his eyes, inhaling deeply.

Josie said the candle would relax him. Fine. He crossed his arms on his chest and dared the damn thing to try.

JOSIE STOOD FROWNING at the back exit when the door jangled and she heard Rick call out her name. Her heart immediately lightened and her step into the store was downright springy. Love potions were great, but the real thing couldn't be beat.

Not that she was in love yet. But she had a serious case of lust.

"Hey," she greeted, her entire body washing over with warmth when Rick made no secret of checking her out from the top of her silk blouse to the heels of her strappy sandals.

"Hey, back. You look amazing."

She sashayed closer, reveling in how his gaze darkened with every step. "Thank you. You look like you had a hard day."

He shrugged, his sexy shoulders straining against his sports coat. "Typical day. But I don't want to talk about police work. I want to look around this shop of yours and see what you sell."

Josie swallowed deeply and, despite her fears, swept her arm toward her merchandise, inviting him to browse at will. She shot back behind the counter, trying to busy herself with entering the day's receipts into her inventory and accounting program while he strolled the store.

"I should be done in a few minutes," she said. "I just have to tally up the big sales. I can keep the small stuff for later."

"Take your time," he said absently, browsing through her candle collection.

Try as she might to concentrate on her end-of-the-day routine, she couldn't help but watch him peruse her inventory. He spent a long time looking through the candles and reading the placards that described the properties and enhancements of each creation.

"Do grapefruit and cypress really help with increasing mental awareness?" he asked.

She smiled. "Yes, they do."

"How did you learn all this stuff?"

"The usual places, I guess. From books, from travel. My mother was an aromatherapist and my grandmother ran a botanica in Port-au-Prince for many years."

"In Haiti?" he asked, justifiably surprised. Ordinarily people emigrated from Haiti, not to it.

She nodded, wondering what her new cop boyfriend of sorts would think if he found out her grandmother was a fake voodoo priestess who saw nothing wrong with stealing the last few coins from the starving population of a Third World country to pay her bills. She suspected he wouldn't like it very much. *She* didn't. "It's weird, I know."

"Have you visited her?"

She shook her head vigorously. "Once, when I was a kid, but honestly the woman creeps me out. She comes here every few years, though, and drags me to every botanica in the state to check out their wares. I like to learn."

Josie held her breath as he opened the glass drawer and pulled out an athame, a gorgeous reproduction she'd bought from a vendor out of Germany. The blade, despite the dulled edge, flashed under the hand-blown glass globe glowing directly above it.

Rick turned, the ceremonial knife held gingerly in his hands.

"Tell me this is a letter opener," he begged, his voice vibrating with a touch of both humor and fear.

She saved her file and came around the counter, shaking her head. "I've heard some people use them that way, yes."

"But that's not what they're for," he ventured.

Moment-of-truth time. Josie gave him a noncommittal shrug. "Nope."

He nodded and carefully placed the weapon back in the drawer. "This isn't an ordinary knickknack shop, is it?" Rick asked.

She didn't reply but let her eyes dart around the store as if the answer was obvious…which it was.

"You cater to…"

"You can say the word, Rick."

"The occult?"

She supposed that description fit, but she certainly didn't like all the negative connotations that had attached themselves to the word. "My clientele are mostly people like you, curious about things that are unusual and are connected to the unexplained. I have Goth kids who stock up on organic black lipstick and I make quite a bit of money from women in the suburbs who use the herbs and dried flowers to make potpourri."

He glanced at the athame. "But I'm betting those Martha Stewart fangirls aren't buying those to use to open their bills from American Express."

"No," she said. "Those are mostly purchased by Wiccans like me who use them to cast a sacred circle."

"A sacred circle?"

"For rituals. It's a space cleansed of negativity where we commune with the god and the goddess."

"And you clean it with a knife?"

Josie heard the rattle of disconcertedness in his voice, but she could also see how hard he was trying to overcome his reluctance of accepting the unknown. Then he took a small step away from her—but he might as well have moved a mile.

"It's part of the ritual. A knife is only one tool to use to free the space of negative energy. In fact, if I was going to clear out my store right this very moment, I'd probably have to pull out my Hoover."

On that snippy comment, Josie returned to her laptop and her receipts. Her fingers jabbed the keys with a little more force than necessary, but the fact of the matter was, she was tired. Tired of being judged for her belief system. Tired of having to explain said belief system to men who, while they'd found her attractive enough when they thought she simply had a somewhat unconventional job and eclectic taste in clothes, freaked out the minute they realized she was a witch.

All this for a man with a badge?

"Look," she said finally, staring straight at Rick, who was now fingering a collection of hand-strung precious-gem necklaces, "I let Lilith borrow my laptop earlier and now I'm behind on my paperwork. Maybe we should get together another night."

Like the twelfth of Never.

Rick frowned. "You sure? I can wait."

Just like a man to miss how angry she was.

She took a deep breath. With her brain unclouded by lust, she pressed her palms flat on the counter and decided to nip this failure of an affair in the bud.

"Can you wait until I become someone else?"

"Excuse me?"

"You know," she said, coming out from behind the counter again, her arms tight across her chest, "until I start wearing conservative clothes and working a normal job and believing in things that don't freak people out."

Rick had the decency to look confused, but Josie knew that after a few minutes reality would set in. Lilith had warned her not to go after men like Rick, men who had lifestyles they'd chosen that were so different from hers. But had she listened? No. Time and time again she pursued men she thought would bring much-needed stability into her life. She kept forgetting that men like Rick wouldn't be so keen on what *she* brought to the table—namely the instability that they fought so hard to keep at bay.

"Did I say something to offend you?" Rick asked.

"Not yet."

Rick shot her a quick grin. "You're still plugged into Lilith's psychic abilities, then? You know that sometime soon I'm going to say something to piss you off?"

"I don't need clairvoyance to know this—" she waved her hand between them "—is destined for failure. I've been fooling myself from the beginning, hoping that maybe you'd like having someone unexpected and unpredictable and, I don't know, different from you in your life."

"You're right."

"But I could see from the way you looked at the knives that you think I'm—what do you mean I'm right?"

Rick shoved his hands into his pockets and rolled back on his heels. "I mean, you're right that I think you're the weirdest woman I've ever met. You're also right that one glance at those potential weapons you keep in those decorative drawers makes the hairs on my arms stand straight up."

"See? We're a waste of time."

"Now that's where you're dead wrong."

"How do you figure?"

"Look, I've been a cop long enough to recognize someone who's on the defensive. You don't really want to listen. You just want me to talk so you can tear down everything I say."

Josie opened her mouth, then popped her lips closed. He was right. "Then I'll talk. I have a record."

"I know. Six counts of petty theft. Four counts of fraud. A bunch of misdemeanors all related to the running of a scam orchestrated by your mother and uncle. The most time you did was four days in county when you were nineteen, though you do have a juvie record that's been sealed."

She swallowed hard. She shouldn't have been surprised that he'd checked her out, but hearing her litany of crimes— at least the ones the cops had charged her with—still stung.

"And you still want to hang out with me?"

Rick shrugged. "Yeah."

Josie crossed her arms. "Don't you wish I'd told you myself?"

"Yeah, but I figured you'd get around to it, which you just

did. We only met yesterday and haven't even been on a real date. We don't know each other."

"You know more about me than I do about you."

"Then let's fix that. Look, Josie, I'm well aware that you don't fit the perfect little picture of my ideal woman, but maybe my picture needs adjustment."

"Doesn't mean you should be working the opposite end of the spectrum."

"Sometimes change comes easier when you just jump in with both feet," he pointed out.

At this, Josie chuckled. That's how she'd gotten out of the grift business with her mother. Cold turkey. Said goodbye, staked her claim to a portion of the family's building in return for her keeping her mouth shut about her family's less-than-honest activities and started her new life.

His attitude stole the angry wind from her defensive sails.

"You realize I'm a witch?" she asked, making sure he understood that she didn't just sell strange stuff in her shop.

"I suspected as much when I saw the altar in your apartment."

"You didn't say anything about it. I figured you didn't notice."

"I'll be honest. I didn't put two and two together until I came into the store and started looking around. You do realize that I'm Catholic?"

She tried to stifle a grin. "No, I had no idea and I didn't want to assume just because of your ethnic background."

He reached into his shirt and pulled out a gold crucifix dangling from an equally gold strong-linked chain.

"Does this make you uncomfortable? Two people of completely different belief systems having…dinner? Maybe sharing a kiss? Maybe more when the time is right? When they each have more than five minutes to adjust to the fact that spiritually they are coming from two entirely different directions?"

Josie frowned. She'd made a lot of assumptions with Rick, based on nothing more than her past experiences. She'd never had a chance to be the judgmental one in a situation before— and she seemed to be relishing the role more than she should. Usually she was judged as a crank the minute someone spied her pentagram necklace or came into the shop completely unaware of the nature of her products. Now she was doing the judging, reacting against Rick first because he was a cop, then because he was a guy and finally because he worshipped differently than she did.

"You know, we probably aren't really so dissimilar," Josie said. "We both believe, at least I assume, that good should be rewarded and evil should be punished—though not by us but by the deity of choice."

"Really?" His question possessed a wealth of honest curiosity.

"You didn't think we were devil worshippers did you?"

"I was hoping not, but there are all those stories…."

Now he was teasing. "What exactly have you heard?"

He took her hand and reeled her closer. "I'll tell you after the appetizers."

"And after the main course?"

His grin, lopsided and ripe with sweet seduction, caused a rumble in her stomach that transcended the need for food. "Dessert, of course. And, trust me, if we each place our orders correctly, this confection will be very sweet and very rich and worth every single calorie."

Josie could practically taste his promise on her tongue and, with a grin, gave him a quick nod, shut down her laptop and grabbed her purse. She may not have psychic powers, but she had a very strong feeling that she and Rick would be watching the sunrise together, both sated and both on the way to a beautiful friendship.

With benefits, of course.

LILITH CLOSED THE BOOK and rubbed her eyes, exhausted. She now knew the way to kill a warlock. Actually, it wasn't hard. Warlocks were mortal and could die the same as any man. Trouble was, they were wily and ruthless. They stalked their prey—witches—with cunning skill and then killed without warning, normally through nonmagical means since warlocks didn't possess powers until after they'd stolen them from their victim. Although, a seasoned warlock could still possess powers stolen from a previous kill.

So Lilith simply had to be on guard. And for now she had the advantage. She knew—or at least suspected—that Boothe Thompson was a bottom-feeding warlock who already had the stolen power to form energy bursts at his disposal. He could kill her, sure, but he certainly couldn't sneak up on her if she stayed alert.

And for all she knew, he thought her psychic powers were fake, just as everyone else did, making her an unlikely target for his attack. On the other hand, a warlock wouldn't take kindly to a witch working with cops. He could attempt to kill her simply to get her out of the way.

Going up against Boothe Thompson alone would be dangerous. And Lilith, while pessimistic and cranky a good part of the time, still liked living very much.

But she couldn't bring herself to call Regina. Not yet. She couldn't risk losing her sister the way she'd lost her mother.

So instead she'd made a call to her aunt Marion, learning

that the protection squads once so prevalent in the witching world had dwindled for lack of volunteers. The ones they did have had been assigned to an organized warlock threat to the north. Regina was, according to Marion, rebuilding the reserves, but for now they didn't have anyone to spare to investigate a single creepy lawyer who may or may not know the significance of his jewelry.

Which meant for now Lilith was on her own.

Lilith glanced at the athame on her altar, knowing the weapon wasn't meant to kill or even draw blood, but beyond the kitchen knives in her cluttered drawer, she wasn't exactly well stocked with weapons. With a knife, she could strike undetected. She'd also have to be very, very close. The thought of burying a blade into another human's flesh sickened her, so she left the Book of Shadows on the table, hoping she still had some ginger ale in the fridge. She had to do what she had to do, but that didn't mean she had to like it.

The knock interrupted her nausea. She was genuinely happy to find Josie on the other side of the door, her blue eyes caught in a dreamy stare.

"Where have you been?" Lilith asked, as if she didn't know. Josie bore all the signs of a woman who had been kissed and kissed well. Flushed skin. Swollen lips. Mussed hair.

"Out with Rick," she said, fluttering inside Lilith's apartment on a cloud of bliss.

"If *out* was so fabulous that you're glowing, then tell me why you're not still *in*."

Josie tossed her purse onto the couch, then followed her bag in a besotted heap. "He wants to take things slowly."

Lilith arched an eyebrow. "Really?"

"From any other man, I'd suspect he was planning the big brush-off. But Rick's an old-fashioned guy. Besides, he was paged. He had to go in to witness an autopsy."

With a blanch, Lilith shut the door and then joined Josie in the living room, sipping her soda. "Yeah, he's old fashioned. Very old fashioned. Does he know you're a witch?"

"Yup," Josie answered confidently.

"And do you know he's—"

"Yup. We talked a lot about religion tonight. And politics and every other off-limits-to-the-newly-dating topic we could think of."

Lilith stifled a laugh. "You two are the rebels of the romance world."

"Aren't we?" Josie asked, impressed with herself. "We don't have sex and we talk for hours about all the stuff that's supposed to be verboten." Her smile reflected utter infatuation. "I think I'm in love."

That declaration sent Lilith straight into the kitchen. She and Mac had pretty much polished off her bourbon, so she dug into the cabinet until she found an old bottle of rum, and snagged a couple of cans of cola and a lime that while spotted with brown outside was likely yummy and sour on the inside. In minutes she had two Cuba Libres ready for immediate consumption and her ginger ale was tossed down the sink.

"Here," Lilith said, handing Josie a tumbler. "We need to celebrate."

Josie held the drink tightly between her hands. "Did you talk to Regina?"

Lilith took a huge swallow. "I couldn't call her." At Josie's indignant look, she explained. "Our mother was murdered by a warlock, okay? I wasn't there, but I saw the whole thing shortly after it happened. In a vision. If only I'd…"

She let her voice drift away. She'd been twelve years old. Even if her premonition had come in time, she couldn't guarantee she could have stopped what she'd seen. Besides, Marion had been convinced Amber knew the attack was imminent, which was how she'd been able to transfer her powers to Regina before the warlock attacked, saving the St. Lyon legacy from dying with her.

Josie leaned forward, placing her hand softly on Lilith's knee. "It's okay. You don't have to explain."

Lilith took another sip of her drink. "No, it's okay. I never talk about this. To anyone. Not even Regina. After it happened, my aunt and I discussed the situation, especially after I told her that I'd seen the attack just after it happened. Since then, I've understood how important Regina is to the family, to the whole witching world. There isn't anyone to take her place right now. No protégé. No daughter being groomed to assume the Guardianship that my family has held for centuries."

"What about you?"

Lilith nearly shot cola out of her nose. "Me? I don't even have the powers I was born with. No one is going to trust me with anything more than I already have. Had," she amended.

Josie sat up straighter and took a long, drawn-out sip. As if she hadn't had a drink in days.

"I'm sorry," Lilith said. "I'm throwing a lot at you all at once."

Josie shook her head emphatically. "No, no. It's okay. I'm glad you trust me enough to tell me. Can't be easy talking about your mother's death."

Lilith slumped in her chair. "It's not."

"You should be telling all this to Mac."

"How can I tell him this? You at least have the lore of Wicca to help you connect all the dots. What you once believed was a fairy tale you now realize is true. Mac doesn't even have the bedtime stories."

Josie's grin was incorrigible. "You can tell him the bedtime stories, Lilith. In bed, too. I'm sure that would soften the blow."

Lilith filed the suggestion away. Wasn't a bad one, actually. "You seem to have sex on the brain."

Josie's grin split her face in half, one happier than the other. "I do. It's wonderful."

"I'm glad things are working out between you and Rick. I never would have predicted it."

Josie knocked back the rest of her drink. "Sometimes the unpredictable stuff is best. So what are you going to do?"

Lilith set down her drink and wandered over to her altar. She lifted the athame into her hands, wondering how to sharpen the blade, wondering how she could possibly stab the weapon into the man's flesh, even if he wasn't entirely a man at all.

"I have no fucking clue," Lilith said finally.

"Because you know you can't do this alone," Josie said.

She was right. Lilith didn't want to do this alone. Talking to Josie had helped, but her friend simply didn't have the knowledge necessary to help her make the right decision. She could call Regina, but she'd not only put her sister in danger, she'd prove to the Council that she was useless.

She needed someone who could strategize. Someone who could formulate a plan and look at the situation from all possible angles.

She needed Mac.

Turning to Josie, Lilith felt her stomach flip-flop as if she were riding a roller coaster rather than considering her options in a lose-lose battle against evil. If she told him, he could help her. If she told him, he'd leave.

Possibly. Maybe.

Then again, maybe not.

He'd said he wanted the whole truth. He'd said he wanted her trust. Mac was a man of honor. Though he could never have anticipated what his request for the truth would really mean, she did believe that he would at least try to keep his word.

She finished her drink, then slipped onto the couch beside Josie. "I don't have a choice, do I?"

"You have lots of choices, sweetie. You simply have to decide which one will get you what you want."

"I want Mac," she admitted.

Josie hugged her close. "Okay, then. Let's figure out a way to get him."

13

WITH A START, MAC'S EYES flew open. He'd fallen asleep? He took a deep breath and tried to remember where he was. Blinking, he gazed around the apartment, but couldn't see anything beyond the blinding light from four dozen candles blazing around the room. The scent of berry and honey filled his nostrils. The hint of cinnamon riding the undertones flashed his memory with images of last night with Lilith. That's why he'd been so tired. So susceptible to sleep.

So where was he now?

With a shake, he realized he was still at his place. The candle Josie had shoved into his hands had burned down substantially, but the damned thing had multiplied.

"What the—"

"Shh. The candles are supposed to relax you."

He heard Lilith's voice, but even after jumping to his feet and spinning around, he caught no sight of her. His apartment was steeped in contrasts of shadows and light. Disoriented, he automatically reached for his weapon—the weapon he'd turned over to the department, along with his badge.

"Lilith?" he asked, still uncertain.

"Yes, it's me. Relax, Mac."

"What is this?"

"A seduction."

He shook his head, trying to clear the fragrance and sleep-induced fog from his brain.

"A what?"

She emerged from the darkness, a bloodred gown of body-hugging silk curving over her frame. Her hair, brushed forward in sexy spikes that fringed her face, captured the light and reflected back mysterious blue-black strands that made her skin appear translucent. With her lips painted crimson, she looked every inch the witch she was.

"A seduction," she repeated. "Don't tell me you've forgotten what that is?"

He shook his head again. Was he dreaming? Lilith was angry with him. No, he was angry with her. He'd wanted answers and she'd blown him off. Hadn't trusted him. Why, then, was she here?

"Is this a dream?"

"I was hoping you'd think so. Might be the only way I'd get you into bed again after how I acted at Josie's shop."

Pinching his skin, he realized he was wide-awake and Lilith was very real—and breathtakingly beautiful. When the slim strap of Lilith's gown slid off her shoulder, his body tightened and every part of him instantly thrummed with need for her.

"You didn't trust me," he said, reminding both of them why this wasn't a good idea, this seduction of hers.

"When I tell you why," she whispered, "you'll understand."

"Tell me."

She shook her finger rhythmically from side to side, her green eyes glistening with the reflection of the firelight. "Not…just…yet."

Standing directly in front of him, she slid her hands up his chest and over his shoulders, twining her fingers behind his neck. With a tug, she lifted herself higher until their lips met. Not a clash of lusty need, but a brush of potent want.

He encircled her slim hips with his hands, unable to keep from touching her. "Then when?"

"Make love to me," she said, her voice dripping with emotion, her eyes wide with sadness.

"You look as if you expect me to say no," he said.

She shook her head. "No, I expect you to say yes. And then, when it's over and I tell you my secret, I expect you to leave."

Air rushed out of his lungs, hot with frustration. "Then you still don't trust me."

Her mouth curved into a frown. "You're wrong. I do trust you, Mac. It's just…make love to me."

In all the time he'd known Lilith he'd never heard her voice so raw, her emotions so close to the surface. He could practically feel them through her skin. Fear. Reluctance. Desire.

Hope.

Her kiss mirrored all that and more. The moment he lowered his head, she grabbed his cheeks and tugged him down. He wrapped his arms around her, pulling her body flush against his, marveling at how petite and fragile she seemed even as she was raking her hands through his hair and darting her tongue against his with wild abandon. For once, neither one knew what the other wanted—except to be filled, to be completed, to be loved.

Mac drew Lilith to the couch, mindful of the heat emanating from the candles. When he broke the kiss, Lilith inhaled deeply.

"Can you smell it?" she asked.

He chuckled and nuzzled her neck. "The cinnamon?"

"The magic. Josie worked hard on these candles. They're supposed to bring clarity."

Mac kissed a path across her shoulder blades. "I'm completely clear on what I want right now."

"But what about tomorrow?"

Mac stared deep into her eyes and wished he had the ability to read her mind the way she had with him in the beginning. Lilith had never worried about tomorrows before, and frankly neither had he. But the moment he'd picked her up on the street outside his neighborhood today he'd known he wanted more than just another fling. He wanted Lilith for the long run, which was why her lack of trust in him had infuriated him. Maybe she needed more time. Maybe she deserved more time. But Mac realized that around her, he was incredibly impatient.

If he wanted her, he'd just have to do whatever it took to get her.

He cupped her face, willing her to read the sincerity in his eyes. "I'll want the same thing tomorrow that I do right this minute, no matter what secret you're keeping."

She pushed him back on the couch and stretched her body across his. "I'm going to take you at your word."

A surge of emotion swelled in Mac's chest, throwing him off with its intensity. For the first time since he'd been with Lilith, tonight would not be just about sex and fantasy and pleasure. He had a chance, finally, to show Lilith how he truly cared for her, how her psychic power or lack thereof didn't mean a damned thing when all was said and done.

The realization struck him dumb, which Lilith took advantage of by kissing him thoroughly.

The silk of her gown felt cool and enticing against his palms. The curves of her backside fit perfectly in his hands, and he relished the feel of her fingers roaming over his body, too, stripping him of his shirt one button at a time. When she spread the material wide and dropped her lips to his chest, he thought his heart would hammer its way out from beneath his ribs.

For a split second they fumbled on the couch, tossing pillows aside carefully to make more room but not knock over any of the candles.

"You know," Lilith whispered, "just once, we might want to start in the bedroom."

Mac chuckled, smoothing his hands over her bare arms, twisting his fingers around the straps, torn over whether or not to remove the lingerie when she looked so incredibly stunning in red. "But you've gone to so much trouble to set the scene right here."

She glanced around. "You don't think it's overkill?"

"With you? Never."

Mac surrendered to his instincts and curved the straps of the gown down her shoulders. He skimmed his fingers over the loosened material, just barely making contact with her breasts. She gasped, and while he reveled in the feel of her mouth on his, he desperately needed to taste her hardened flesh.

Shifting their positions, he tugged the material down just enough to reveal her dark areola and puckered nipple. She cooed as he suckled, and he intensified her reactions by pinching her other breast softly, just enough to blend the pressure with the pain of pure pleasure. Emboldened by her gasps, he guided her back until he was over her, alternating his attention from one breast to another, loving her with his hands, teeth and tongue until her gasps turned to tiny pants. She was on the brink. On the edge. He continued until she crested, then kissed her cries away.

"That's…not…fair," she said once the trembling subsided.

He swirled sweet circles over her nipples with his thumbs. "Turnabout is fair play," he teased.

Her laughter brought his attention back to her breasts, sweetly bruised pink, a stunning contrast next to the red silk of her gown. When he moved in to take another taste, she slipped her arms back into her straps. "Oh, no, you don't. I need time to regroup. It's my turn to torture you now."

And torture she did. First, she undressed him. Slowly. So slowly Mac thought he might turn inside out in his need to separate himself from his skin and slip fully into hers. Then she kissed him all over, missing not a single inch of flesh. She paid extra attention to his backside, teasing between his thighs with her finger, smearing her crimson lipstick over his body, leaving a red-hot trail, marking him as hers. When she finally gave him back the reins of their lovemaking, he wanted to do nothing more than drive inside her and pump them both to madness.

He had his chance when she climbed onto his lap and smoothed her moist labia over his sex, then guided him inside her, cooing as his hard shaft slicked into her. She stopped long enough to position the gown so it flowed around them. He'd never seen anything so sexy in his life. He could feel the bareness of her body, but he couldn't see a thing.

Her movements started off slow, languorous yet precise. Her hips undulated. Her hands roamed. It was all he could do to lean his head back and revel in the sensations coursing through him. She stretched and swiveled until all the blood in his body rushed toward her and her amazing ministrations. She coaxed and teased, moaned and cooed, firing him until he couldn't help but splay his hands on her hips and quicken the pace. Just when he thought he'd tumble, she stopped, pushed off him and darted toward the bedroom.

After taking a minute to regain his balance, Mac followed. He shouldn't have been surprised that she'd placed several candles around his bed, but he was. When she flipped one strap of her gown off her shoulder, he grabbed the doorjamb. His dick throbbed with wanting, but still he watched as she oh-so-slowly peeled her gown off, then stepped out of the crimson pool and climbed languidly across his mattress.

"Why did you stop?" he asked, joining her on the bed.

She speared her hands into his hair, allowing her pinkies to tease the sensitive edges of his ears. "I don't know," she said with surprising shyness, "I just wanted to lie down with you. To feel you on me and inside me completely."

Mac didn't deny her. He stripped away the comforter beneath them and pulled away the sheets, positioned her among the pillows, then slipped inside her. Stirred by the glossiness in her bright green eyes, he clasped his hands on either side of her face and watched as the rapture of their love-making overtook her.

He'd never witnessed anything so beautiful in his life. The way her mouth parted to accommodate tiny gasps of breath. The way she moistened her lips with her tongue. The way her head rocked from side to side as the passion built and expanded. His own skin flared with the knowledge that he could affect her so deeply, that he could chase away her demons even if only for a few minutes of bliss.

God, he loved her. He loved everything about her. He wanted nothing more than to share this love for the rest of his life. On that thought alone, he came. And soon after, she joined him, shocking the hell out of him when instead of tumbling passionately into orgasm, she squealed in delight.

"DO IT AGAIN!"

Shock gave way to laughter. "Now that's what I like to hear."

"No," Lilith said, her entire body bubbling with excitement so that her heart tapped an exhilarated beat in her ears. "Think something."

Mac's eyebrows popped up. "What?"

"Think something," she said. "Anything."

"Did you hear what I was thinking just before?" he asked, clearly reluctant.

Lilith could barely control the burst of uninhibited joy ricocheting through her. "I love you!"

Amid a burble of mutual laughter, Mac kissed her hard and long. With their bodies still slick with sweat, the friction sparking between them nearly made her forget what had just happened. Nearly but not quite.

"I love you, too," he said once he yanked his lips off her. He went in for another kiss, but Lilith blocked him, placing her hand over his mouth.

"I know," she said, giggling.

She was giggling. Good goddess. Every inch of her skin flared with electricity, but naked with Mac on top of her, she didn't know if the reaction was from him or from regaining her powers or from discovering that he loved her with all his heart and soul. Probably a combination of all three. If she didn't know for a fact that she didn't have the power, she might have floated to the ceiling.

He kissed her again, still completely oblivious to the full meaning of what she'd just told him. She knew he loved her not because of cocky overconfidence but because she'd heard his thoughts as if she'd spoken them herself.

The only message she was receiving now had to do with

another round of sizzling-hot sex. And while Lilith didn't object to the idea, she had to be sure she wasn't mistaken.

With a playful shove, she moved out from underneath Mac, leaving him to bounce on the mattress, confused.

She grabbed the top sheet and wrapped it around her body, hoping that covering up might help him regain his thought processes. "Did you hear what I said? I know that you love me."

"You should," he said. "Not only did I do a rather fine job of showing you, I told you."

"No, you didn't."

"Yes, I—"

She waved her hand. "You never actually *said* the words. Not until I said them first."

"But…"

Luckily for her, Mac was a sharp guy. The expression on his face told her that the fog of lust had faded from his brain, and that he fully realized just what she'd said.

"You can read my mind."

She couldn't help bouncing on her toes. "Yes! My powers are back."

He frowned so hard Lilith thought he might break the muscles in his face. She tried hard not to seep into his mind. She knew he didn't want her there, and while she wasn't yet adept at keeping out of where she wasn't invited, she was determined to try. For Mac.

"How?"

She twirled around in a circle, the sheet flaring happily around her. "I have no idea. But do it again. Think something. Think something I could never guess in a million years."

Mac's eyes glistened with reluctance.

"I promise," she said, taking his hand, kissing the palm,

then pressing his flesh to her face. "I will not invade your mind uninvited. Ever."

After a tense moment, he closed his eyes.

Lilith waited for the words.

They didn't come.

Her heart dropped like a bowling ball into the pit of her stomach.

"Are you thinking?" she asked.

"Yes," he replied without opening his eyes.

Maybe she was rusty? After less than a week? Wait. Maybe she'd blocked him inadvertently, knowing how much he detested her ability when focused on him. Concentrating, she pulled back a visual curtain in her mind and, behind the deep red velvet, caught the image of a photograph.

"You're thinking about a couple. Your parents. They're…" Lilith's voice caught in her throat as the picture revealed itself fully. The man dashing in a tuxedo. The woman radiant in resplendent ivory lace. "Getting married."

Mac's eyes flashed open. "You know, my father told me that he married my mother because of her looks, but he couldn't help it if she was such a great—"

"Cook!" she shouted triumphantly.

Mac's eyes widened and Lilith laughed, realizing she wanted to meet his parents. She wanted to know his family. She wanted them to know her. She couldn't imagine them liking her—but, hey, one step at a time. She sat on the bed, wanting to know more about Mac in every way but closing the curtain in her mind anyway.

"That's sweet," she commented.

"What I mean is," Mac said, drawing a soft line down her chin, "I don't love you because you're psychic, but it's part of the deal. I plan to make the best of it, even if I'll never pull off a decent surprise gift for you."

"That's not necessarily the case." She reached across the mattress and placed her hand over his. "I can block you."

"Are you blocking me right now?"

She nodded.

He smiled slyly. "Good, because if you weren't, you'd probably slap the shit out of me for what I'm thinking about right now. There's this one fantasy we never tried before. Has to do with a French maid—"

Lilith popped him in the shoulder, on principle alone. "You're dreaming, Mancusi."

"What a shame. You can really block me?"

"Of course. If I didn't have the ability to block, I'd go insane hearing each and every thought of every person in the city. Blocking is one of the first skills a psychic learns."

"Why didn't you tell me?"

"You mean before? Would you have believed me?"

"Doubtful."

"Exactly. From the moment you realized what I could do until you left was approximately ten minutes."

"I was a fool."

"Yeah, you were. But I was, too. I shouldn't have used my abilities to manipulate you. When it all started, I had no idea we'd—"

"Fall in love?"

"Now who's reading whose mind?"

His smile nearly blinded her. "Maybe we can make this work."

Lilith curled into his body, and he wrapped himself around her in a cocoon of emotion she thought would smother her but instead warmed her to the core. "We can, but first we need to finish what we've started."

He started peeling the sheet away. "I'm all for that."

She laughed and slapped his hungry hands. "That's not what I meant. The Council must have given me a reprieve because of Po—"

From the other room they heard the trill of Mac's cell phone. Lilith nearly whooped with joy, having sensed the call coming in before the sound alerted them.

"Answer it," she encouraged. "Rick has news about Pogo's autopsy."

With only a flash of uncertainty in his eyes, Mac hustled out of his bedroom in all his naked glory. Giving herself only a moment to enjoy the tight curve of his impressive backside, she hunted for her clothes. She jumped into her panties, then fished out the workout pants and jacket she'd shoved in her bag so she could seduce Mac in the bold red nightgown—the one she'd lost somewhere during the evening. Once she cleared out the clothes, she found the books she'd also placed in the bag. She'd realized that the time had come for her to lay all her cards on the table for Mac. Even now that she'd regained her powers, she knew she had no choice but to tell him the whole truth about herself, demons—literally—and all. Then he could make his choices. Then he could decide if he wanted to trade the enamored couple in the photograph for the two of them.

"You're sure?" Mac asked into the phone as Lilith eased into the room. "What does the ME think?"

Lilith rolled her eyes. She could about guarantee that no medical examiner had a clue what had caused Pogo's death.

"Are they consulting with the FBI?"

Lilith snorted. More letters wouldn't help. Of course, for all she knew, the government intelligence agency had a file on unexplained deaths that could all be traced back to magic. Wouldn't that make Regina happy.

Regina. If the Council knew about the warlock and had returned her powers in order to help her fight him, wouldn't Regina have been alerted? And wouldn't she have immediately sought out Lilith, no matter where she was?

This was odd.

Mac disconnected his call.

"You were right about the autopsy."

"Of course I was," she said, breaking away from her thoughts of her sister to open the book to the page on warlocks. "I also know what killed Pogo."

She turned the book so he could see the line drawing of the intensely angry-looking warlock.

"Who is that?"

"*What* is a better question. It's a warlock."

"Isn't that a male witch?"

She shivered visibly. "That's a huge misconception. Male witches are still witches. Warlocks are evil, power-sucking creatures. They kill witches in order to steal their abilities."

Confused, Mac sat beside her on the couch, clearing candles out of the way to slide the text closer to him. "You think one of these killed Pogo?"

"I'm pretty certain. Pogo's body bore the signs of being killed with an energy burst, a concentrated ball of electricity that passes through the skin and electrocutes the internal organs of the body. On mortals, it doesn't leave a visible mark."

"That's why you wanted to see Pogo's body," he suggested.

She nodded. "I had to be sure."

"So you think Pogo Goins was a witch?"

"No way."

"How does one…recognize…a witch?"

Lilith had to think. Could she have identified a witch with active powers when hers were down?

"I'm not sure," she admitted. "But he'd have to have listed his name with the Registry if he was, and I already checked him out. There's no listing."

"The Registry?"

Lilith took a deep breath and exhaled slowly. She was throwing a lot at Mac all at once. First and foremost, admitting her feelings for him. That had been hard enough. Now she was risking her powers again by explaining the full and true nature of her world. Would the Council again take her clairvoyance from her? She couldn't be sure they were the reason her power had come back in the first place, but she had already told Josie quite a bit with no negative consequences. She simply had to take a chance.

"The Registry is a place in Arizona where all active-power witches on the North American continent must go to register with the Council. My sister, Regina, is the Guardian, which means she's responsible for the Registry."

Mac dragged his hands through his hair. "We're talking about more here than Wiccans wearing pentagrams and worshipping the moon, aren't we?"

"Did you Google *Wicca?*"

He looked down sheepishly. "I just wanted to know what I was getting into."

She laid her head on his shoulder. "That's so sweet," she cooed, then straightened, tapping the book. "But, yeah, this isn't about Wicca. Wicca is the religion practiced by witches, but most Wiccans are mundane practitioners who have no idea about things such as warlocks, demons and hunters."

"Hunters?"

She tapped the book. "Forget about hunters. We're dealing with warlocks. Concentrate."

She ignored his dirty look and explained about how warlocks were conceived, what their purpose was and how they attacked. Then she showed him the symbol in the book and a printout of the enlarged picture of Boothe Thompson's ring.

"You think Boothe Thompson is a warlock?"

She lifted her shoulders and winced. "I think the signs are all there. And if we don't act fast, he could kill again."

"I thought you said warlocks kill witches. Is he after you?"

"I'm not sure. But there's only one way to find out."

14

MAC'S SCOWL COMPETED with the look on the face of the warlock in the Book of Shadows for most horrifying expression. And won. He grabbed both of her hands and squeezed tightly.

"I won't allow you to put yourself in danger."

She arched an eyebrow, hoping her look would squelch whatever wild images were coursing through his brain— starting with the concept that he could *allow* her or *not allow* her, as the case may be, to do anything.

He loosened his grip. "A man can't let the woman he loves walk knowingly into danger, Lilith. It's not how things work."

Her indignation softened. Not enough to let him boss her around, but enough to let the topic drift to the background for a bit. "First, we have to make sure my suspicions are correct. To say the least, all I've amassed so far is circumstantial evidence against Thompson. Pogo died just outside a bar we know Boothe Thompson frequents often enough that no one reacts to his Lamborghini being parked outside. And he wears a ring that screams warlock. I did some checking tonight before I came over. That crescent diamond is rare, but infamous. They were once worn by a coven of warlocks who operated out of guess where."

"Italy?"

The man was on the ball, that was for sure.

Lilith wished she would have paid better attention to her lessons as a young witch. She might have understood the significance of the ring earlier, without having to spend time contacting an old friend at the Registry who would give her the information without alerting her sister.

"Warlocks usually take great pains to hide their true nature in case they happen upon a witch they aren't ready to attack," she explained. "But these warlocks, called the *Collettivo*, were known for showing off. Witches fled Italy in fear."

"I'm sure that made the locals very happy."

She smirked. "The warlocks had nothing to do with the mundanes, trust me. They hunt witches, but they aren't hunters."

"Hunters?"

"A class of mundanes who take it upon themselves to rid the world of witches. They operate on the fringe. Very nasty guys. Trust me on this."

Mac took a deep breath, and Lilith pressed her lips tightly together, knowing she was throwing a lot at him at once. But if he was going to help her, he had to understand the big picture. "The witching world takes great pains to stay uninvolved in the mundane world, even as we live in it. Our battles are fought in secret. No one wants to risk being exposed to the mundanes, who would, as history tells us, hunt us all down—good or bad."

Lilith paused, trying to give Mac time to process all she'd said so far, which was quite a lot. She hadn't realized until now that despite her less-than-attentive practices in school, she might be qualified to teach Witch History at the Registry. Apparently, a lot of Regina's constant studying rubbed off on Lilith when she thought she wasn't paying attention.

Mac stood and paced. She assumed this was a good sign, but had to fight the urge to slip into his mind for a minute and figure out what he was thinking. She took a deep breath and concentrated on the red velvet curtain. She visualized the ropes that opened and closed it and, in her mind, snipped them in half.

"If Thompson is a warlock," Mac said, surprising her, "wouldn't he have attacked you by now? You met him before you lost your powers. You are clairvoyant. Why wouldn't he have killed you to take your power?"

"Maybe he doesn't want that particular gift," she guessed. "It's a hard power to wrangle and warlocks aren't patient."

"You met him before your power was stripped. Why didn't you recognize him as a warlock then?"

That part bothered Lilith. She'd like to think her clairvoyance at the very least would have alerted her to the presence of such a dangerous being, but she'd always come up blank around Thompson. She figured it was because he was such an adept liar. Or perhaps there was more to the magic he'd stolen.

"Witches don't run into warlocks every day. Most can go their entire lifetimes without crossing paths with one. They aren't common and neither are witches. Maybe he chose not to reveal himself to me because he didn't need or want my powers. The *Collettivo* operated so brilliantly in Italy because they hid out in the open, taking positions of power and prestige—power and prestige they attained by stealing from witches." Lilith then considered another possibility, the one that kept her from alerting Regina right away. "I'm the sister of the Guardian. Any attack on me would have brought down all the protection squads. He would have been rooted out and destroyed before he had whatever he wanted, which is clearly more than just the ability to read minds. Thompson might have decided that the best way to fly under the radar is to keep his activities quiet."

Mac stalked around the room, seemingly oblivious to the mess around them. Four dozen burned out candles. Clothes. A wineglass or two. They'd had quite the party earlier, and Lilith's blood heated at the memories, the most unforgettable being her invasion into Mac's mind just as he realized how deeply he loved her.

For a split second she allowed the enveloping wet warmth to surround her again, to ward off the chill from what she might have to do to expose Boothe Thompson and protect her world.

"What kind of activities are we talking about here?" Mac asked, his mind clearly more focused than hers. "Why would a warlock set up shop in Chicago? Is there a large concentration of witches here?"

Lilith shook her head. "Not more than in any other big city. But what Chicago does have in abundance is corruption and crime."

Mac skewered her with an indignant look. "Not more than in any other big city."

She winced. Not a good move to imply to the Chief of Detectives that his city has more criminal activity than others.

"Touché," she quipped. "But no matter what city he chose, he's up to no good. Look at his client list. Chicago has a lot of money to be made in the mundane underworld, where Thompson seems to be dipping his wick quite a bit lately. Taking on the cases of all sorts of lowlifes and their high-life bosses. Defending corrupt politicos and known kingpins. And bottom-feeders like Goins. The only thing I can think is that he's not after witch power at all. At least not yet. He's on a mundane power trip. Money, prestige, influence."

"But is this related to the drugs?"

She shook her head. So much speculation and supposition, she might as well not have regained her powers for all the help they were giving her. "You said the shipment was huge. If he's in on the deal, he could add millions to his coffers and…" She hated to go in such a conspiracy theorist direction, but Lilith knew that warlocks had no limits to their evil. If they'd murder a Guardian in front of her sixteen-year-old daughter as they had with her mother, wouldn't they be low enough to try and manipulate the mundane world until they became so untouchable they could expose witches and kill them without suffering consequences? "What better way to build an army than to coke them up? You said the rumor was that the cocaine wasn't pure. What if it's tainted with something? Maybe even something magical? What if that's what Pogo knew? What if that is the knowledge that got him killed?"

Mac dropped onto the couch again, his eyes wide. "Is that possible, tainting drugs with magic?"

Lilith buried her face in her hands, then stabbed her fingers through her hair, tugging on the roots, willing her brain to work harder and faster. "I don't know, Mac. But I've seen potions do remarkable things, so I have to guess that, yes, it is."

MAC LEANED BACK AGAINST the couch cushions, his brain swimming with information he had no idea how to process. It had been hard enough to come to terms with Lilith having true paranormal abilities. Now he learned that not only was there a whole race of paranormal witches out there, but there was also a separate nation of enemies who wanted their powers and would be more than willing to kill to get them.

"I know I've dumped a lot on you," Lilith said.

Mac swore softly. "Yeah. I don't even know how to put this all together into something that makes sense."

Lilith lifted the book off the table and laid it in Mac's lap. "Read this. This is a Book of Shadows written by a witch who worked on a protection squad in Mexico about a hundred years ago."

"You mentioned them earlier. You have those?"

Lilith stood and stretched, then answered him with a nod and a yawn.

"Then why aren't you calling them?" he asked, knowing she was exhausted because they'd stayed up half the night making love. Over and over and over. More than anything in the world, he wanted to strip her bare, tug her into his arms, hustle her back to bed and forget that her world and his were about to collide in ways that could change more than just their lives and their futures. Mac couldn't deny that since Boothe Thompson had risen to the top of the defense-attorney heap, crime had skyrocketed in the city. Part of the reason the old mayor had lost his bid for reelection had been the growing wave of unpunished illegal activity.

What if Boothe Thompson *had* somehow fed the crime wave as part of some grand design?

And yet, despite all that, the question foremost in his mind revolved around when he and Lilith would make love again. That was how a couple should celebrate the mutual admission of love, right? Uninterrupted lusty hot sex for hours on end? Instead they were talking about energy bursts, warlocks and…what was it called? A Book of Shadow? "I hate to admit this, babe, but I have a feeling this shit is out of my league."

With a grin that melted him from the inside out, Lilith reached down and patted his cheek, then stroked his skin, her eyes brimming with sensual promise. "I sincerely doubt that. Read how you kill a warlock. It's right up your alley. Besides, once I'm sure that Thompson is a warlock, I'll call in the big wands, so to speak. The protection squads aren't as numerous as they once were. If I call for help now, Regina will come—and, to be honest, I'm deathly afraid that she's the one he's after."

Not calling for backup went against Mac's training, but he also knew that a good cop didn't call in a code 10-1—officer needs assistance—until the first responder assessed the situation thoroughly.

And to do that, they needed to find Boothe Thompson.

"If you meet with Thompson now, with your powers back, will you be able to tell what he's up to?"

Lilith looked up at him, hypnotic green eyes dark with uncertainty. "I don't know. I've never been able to read him, but if he's a warlock who's stolen the power to block me, I might find a way around his walls."

"Sounds dangerous," Mac said, his chest tightening. Having Lilith follow Boothe Thompson on the freeway was one thing. Having her confront him when he might have the power to kill her in a way Mac couldn't prevent was something else altogether.

Lilith scooted across the couch and took both of Mac's hands in hers. She stared at him for a long moment, then abandoned the sweet and tender posture and jumped into his lap, slid her hand into his hair and nuzzled against his neck, trailing hot kisses across his flesh.

"Living is dangerous," she assured him. "Loving is dangerous. And yet I'm willing to put myself on the line to do those two things to be with you. What's one more risk?"

Mac surrendered to her kiss, unable and unwilling to resist the temptation Lilith brought into his life. He'd been a cop for going on twenty years. He'd faced danger in all forms and under every type of situation imaginable.

Or at least he'd thought so until a few hours ago.

The melding of their mouths injected him with a hot surge of emotion. Was it fear? Love? Desire? Anticipation? Perhaps a combination of all four? He loved Lilith. He'd already admitted as much both to her and to himself. But in loving her, could he let her take on the task she'd clearly been born for?

He wasn't sure, but he knew that soon, one way or another, he'd find out.

"Anything else you can tell me, Mr. Thompson?"

Thompson glanced up from the file on his desk with cool precision, his blue eyes sharp with annoyance. This was a look meant to dismiss, and Thompson had it down pat.

"No, Detective Fernandez. Rest assured I've given you all the information you require."

Lilith concentrated but had no trouble conjuring the image and sound of Rick's interview with Boothe Thompson. She'd become a regular human surveillance system. Actually, witch surveillance. Either way, she'd managed to plug into the action down the hall with little difficulty, thanks to Det. Fernandez's willing and open mind. Not only had her powers returned, but they were back with a vengeance. She could only hope that Thompson, if he really was a warlock, couldn't sense what she and Mac were up to.

They'd accompanied Rick up to Thompson's office for an after-hours interview of the wily attorney, who'd avoided meeting with police for two days since Pogo's murder, claiming to be tied up in court. In the meantime, Goins's body had been cremated. The medical examiner had had no choice but to rule the death accidental, and Goins's girlfriend had insisted on putting the matter to rest. Permanently. Didn't matter one way or another to Lilith if they couldn't establish the real cause of death. Even if she proved Thompson was a warlock who'd thrown an energy burst to kill Goins, she'd make her case only to herself and the Council. The mundane police could never, ever know.

Except for Mac. And surprisingly, Rick. She'd been shocked when Mac had shared her theory with the young detective, figuring Mac would rather not have his subordinates think that he was suffering from some sort of postsuspension dementia. But as Mac had guessed, Rick took the news in relative stride. He'd had Josie to help him understand, of course. The two of them were as sweet, as connected and as mismatched as the two sides of a black-and-white cookie. If Lilith hadn't been such a die-hard cynic, she would have declared them monstrously cute and destined for an enduring love affair, if not lifelong commitment.

"Rick's leaving," she warned, and seconds later the door to Boothe's office opened and Rick shuttled out.

"Do shut the door behind you," Thompson instructed.

Rick obeyed, then with a gesture that resembled a friendly wave, shot him the bird.

He joined Lilith and Mac in the conference room they'd snuck into. After eight o'clock, the law office had long since closed. Only Boothe Thompson and a few clerks in the offices one floor below remained.

"Anything?" Rick asked her.

Lilith shook her head. She'd hoped to get a bead on Thompson's involvement in Pogo's death, but she'd witnessed nothing of use. Thompson was still a blank page to her, at least through Rick's eyes.

"I know you have a serious hankering for some deep dish tonight," she quipped.

Rick stared at her, his expression somewhere between shock and indignation. "I hope that's—"

She raised her hand. "Let's assume you mean pizza. Trust me, I don't want to go there any more than you do." She kept her voice low, then motioned to Rick to close the door all the way. She sensed suspicion somewhere nearby. Possibly from Thompson. Or someone else.

"My powers must be increasing," she concluded. "I've never been able to eavesdrop on a conversation in another room before."

"Have you tried?" Mac asked.

"Duh," she said. "More times than I can count. Today, it was almost a snap. Helped that Rick was willing."

"But Thompson wasn't," Rick added.

Lilith tried to picture the scene in Thompson's office now but saw nothing but darkness in her mind. "Maybe if I get closer."

"No," Mac said decisively. "It's too dangerous. We need to arrange for you to bump into Thompson in a public place. That way you can get close, but he wouldn't dare try to harm you."

"He's going to the mayor's reception tonight," Rick informed them. "I think that's why he allowed me the quick interview. He didn't want me harassing him at the party."

"Where's the reception?" Mac asked.

"Some contributor's house. I'm sure the chief is invited,

so I'll find out the details. I'll get back to you. Now let's blow this joint, because if we get busted, I lose my badge."

Rick left first, giving them the all-clear just as the elevator doors swung closed. Mac and Lilith exited down the hall, deciding to take the stairs two floors up and then catch another elevator down. Mac had his hand on the door to the stairwell when a deep-throated chuckle sounded from behind them.

"Detective Mancusi," Boothe Thompson said, his voice ripe with gloating. "I give you a gift in not insisting you lose your job for attacking me, and this is how you repay my generosity of spirit—by sneaking around my offices?"

Lilith closed her eyes tightly, trying to penetrate the blackness surrounding Boothe Thompson's aura. Unable to part the curtain of shadow, she turned. Mac did so, as well, subtly positioning himself in front of her.

"We were tailing Detective Fernandez," Mac lied. "This has nothing to do with you."

Thompson smirked. "You expect me to believe that?"

Lilith tried again, this time keeping her eyes open. Her vision swirled with tendrils of psychic energy reaching out and around Thompson, trying to coax his true nature free.

"What are you?" she asked, her voice a whisper.

But in the eerie silence of the deserted hallway, the question rang out loud and clear.

Thompson grinned ear to ear. "I'm exactly what you fear most. Someone immune to your psychic abilities, if you still had them. But you've been stripped clean, haven't you? A fallen witch. A waste of oxygen and space in this crowded city, if you asked me."

He didn't know. He had no idea that Lilith's powers had returned. Not that they were of any use to her. Still, she embraced the air of safety descending around her. If Thompson was a warlock, he would not try to take powers he did not know existed. If he wasn't, he knew quite a bit about witchcraft that he shouldn't. But he wouldn't kill her. Not when her death would bring down the wrath of the Guardian.

Unless that's what he wanted? A war?

"You know nothing about me," she challenged, though she wondered how anyone but a warlock could know the little he did. Unless he was…a witch?

"Don't play the fool. How would I know about your powers being stripped if I wasn't connected to all the right people?"

"Trust me," Lilith quipped, "none of the 'right' people know a thing about me."

"Except your sister?"

Lilith's gasp was covered by the sound of the elevator slicing open directly to Boothe's right. He instinctively turned toward the sound and Mac took the same advantage. Spinning, he grabbed her arm and pushed her toward the door to the stairs.

"Get out of here," he ordered.

She yanked herself out of his grip. "I'm not going to run," she insisted.

"DETECTIVE MANCUSI? What are you doing here?"

Mac spun, his hand hovering over the .38 he'd shoved into his jacket. He might have lost his badge and his department-issued firearm, but he still had a license to carry and a strong survival instinct, even if the chances of his suspension ever being lifted now dropped to zero.

"Mr. Mayor."

Perkins Dafoe straightened the jacket of his tuxedo. The

entourage usually clucking behind him was nowhere to be seen, but the ire on his boss's face was front and center.

Mac felt Lilith shift behind him. When Dafoe's face reddened, he knew the jig was completely up.

"And you!"

Lilith stepped directly to Mac's left. "Looking very dapper, Mayor Dafoe."

The mayor turned completely to Thompson. "What's going on here? I ordered these two to stay away from you."

Thompson gave them a cursory glance, bowing slightly when he addressed Dafoe.

"You're early, sir," Thompson said.

Ignoring the glare Defoe shot at them, Lilith tried to read the man. He was a jumble of thoughts and emotions, an incomprehensible swirl of images that moved at lightning speed and nearly made her dizzy. She was forced to grab Mac's arm to keep upright.

And her stomach ached as if someone had just punched her hard in her midsection. She fought to keep from doubling over.

Lies. Lies. Lies.

"We had business here," Mac said, "but not with Mr. Thompson, since you ordered me to stay away from him."

The sarcasm in Mac's voice wasn't lost on either Lilith or the mayor, who narrowed his eyes accusingly. "I should have been more specific and included Mr. Thompson's place of business."

Mac gave an innocent shrug. "The devil's in the details."

The mayor snapped a look at Thompson. "We're late for the benefit. And they're getting in my way too often. Get rid of them."

"We were just leaving," Mac said, motioning Lilith toward the stairwell door again.

The mayor started toward Thompson's office, stopped, grinned haughtily at Mac, then repeated his order to Thompson. "You know too much, don't you, Ms. St. Lyon?"

The ribbons of energy around the mayor swirled dark. First red, then purple, then black.

Lilith swallowed her gasp. Thompson wasn't the warlock—the mayor was.

She made the realization just as Thompson extended his hand, the palm sparking with the impending energy burst.

Lilith tore down the curtain between her mind and Mac's, then grabbed his shirt and yanked him back into the stairwell with her. The energy burst struck impotently against the metal door. Mac's fear for her life nearly overwhelmed her, but she needed his guidance. She had to know what to do before he had to ask her.

"Run!"

Mac had his weapon drawn, but Lilith tore down the stairs two at a time, diving under the landing as another burst exploded above their heads.

"He's not a warlock," Lilith told Mac, panting as they caught their breath. "He's a witch. A rogue black witch. I never thought—"

Another fireball. Mac shot to the door from the next floor and yanked it open. Lilith bolted through, electricity sparking all around as the burst impacted against the metal of the stairs, singeing her skin.

The floor was deserted, offering them several places to hide. Mac chose the nearest conference room. He'd have a clear shot through the glass. But Lilith feared what would happen to his career if he killed Boothe Thompson in his own office space. For all intents and purposes, Thompson was unarmed. If Mac killed the lawyer, he'd be arrested, tried and convicted for cold-blooded murder. The mayor would see to the judgment, since he—a warlock—was clearly in cahoots with the traitorous witch.

Lilith pulled out the athame she'd slid into the back of her jeans. Mac grabbed her by the wrist.

"What are you doing?"

"You can't kill him," she said. "You'd never be able to prove self-defense."

Mac pulled her behind the door separating the conference room from the hallway. "The mayor ordered the hit. How are we going to get out of here if I don't shoot the bastard?"

Lilith saw his fear in his mind, and every quake and shiver was for her. He knew he could make the shot, knew with every fiber of his being that he was willing to pay the ultimate price as long as Lilith escaped unscathed. But she couldn't allow him to sacrifice himself for her. Not now. Not ever.

They heard the door from the stairwell to the hallway creak open.

Lilith closed her eyes and concentrated. With her powers increasing, she had to take a chance. She telegraphed a distress signal to Rick, who'd opened his mind to her only minutes before. Could he return in time? If he showed up, at least there would be a witness.

Thompson's overconfident chuckle echoed through the hallway.

"You've no place to go, unless your witch has a broomstick and can fly you down twenty-four flights."

He laughed at the hilarity of his statement.

Lilith rolled her eyes.

I'd like a broomstick right now to shove up his...

Mac glanced at her sharply, his eyes wide with warning.

Had he heard her thought?

Uh-oh.

This was a new turn of events.

She concentrated, tried again.

I love you.

Mac grinned and returned the thought. Literally.

Telepathy?

Cool.

"Do us all a favor," Thompson said, his voice growing louder as he neared. "Come out and I'll kill you both quickly. I'll attend your memorials and make sure your families understand how much everyone loved you both. Yes, Lilith, even your family. I know someone who is quite anxious to meet your sister."

Stay still, Mac warned. The man had great reflexes, even in his brain. She'd barely moved her pinkie finger, but she'd been seconds away from intercepting Thompson, perhaps drawing his fire. While she was a little rusty, she did have experience dodging energy bursts.

Mac tightened his hand around her upper arm.

Don't even think about it.

She glared at him. *I can distract him.*

And then what?

Neither had time to think an answer, much less say it out loud. An energy burst crashed into the room, shattering the glass next to them. Acting entirely on instinct, Mac fired his weapon three times. Thompson screamed, then dropped to the ground.

Mac jumped out of their hiding space and ordered Lilith

to retreat while he checked on the lawyer. Thompson writhed in pain, blood oozing from his right hand and left shoulder.

"Don't get too close," Lilith warned. She guessed the wounds would keep Thompson from attacking again, but she couldn't be sure. Not when Thompson practiced the dark arts—which he must have if he was in cahoots with a warlock. He hadn't stolen the power to make the bursts. It had been his to begin with.

Mac kept as safe a distance as possible while he checked Thompson's pulse and tried to staunch the bleeding in his shoulder.

"You won't live to celebrate my death," Thompson croaked.

"Did you kill Pogo?" Mac asked, his voice emotionless.

"He knew too much."

"About the drugs?"

Thompson's laugh was hollowed by pain. "It's too late. We've already moved half the stash. You'll never stop us…from…taking…"

The lawyer lost consciousness.

Mac cursed. "Call 911."

Lilith moved back inside the conference room when she felt the increasing menace reaching out to them. Black ribbons of evil snatched her around the neck, tightening slowly but effectively. She tried to turn to Mac, but the ribbons compressed her. She could barely breathe.

Mac.

"Call the ambulance," Mac said again, his eyes darting to the stairwell door and the elevator.

He's coming for us, she thought, then dropped to her knees, gasping.

Immediately Mac was at her side. As if she were trapped

in a wind tunnel, she heard Mac's voice calling out to her. Or was it his thoughts? Life choked out of her, breath by untaken breath. Mac grabbed her shoulders and spun her out of the way just in time to see the mayor standing over Boothe Thompson, his hands extended as he sucked the powers—and the life—out of his partner.

Lilith used the shift in the mayor's focus to concentrate on breaking free. She gripped Mac's hand until she thought she'd fracture her fingers and followed his voice out of the tangle of asphyxiating ribbons. She gasped, able to breathe again, just as Thompson expired.

Perkins Dafoe turned to them, exposed, a bitter smile on his face.

"Such a shame," he said of the now-dead witch. "So far as minions went, he was very effective. A little showy, a little flashy. The ring was overkill, but I'll miss his presence as I climb the ladder to true power."

He glanced down at the palms of his hands, which sparked with the new ability he'd stolen from Thompson, giving Lilith one chance to act. Usurping power wasn't as easy as the drain. Perkins Dafoe might possess the power to form an energy burst now, but he likely didn't have the skill.

On that realization, Mac raised his weapon. Dafoe shifted and with a wave of his hand, now no longer electrified, tele-kinetically yanked it from Mac's grip. As Mac dived after the lost gun, Lilith darted forward, her brain focused on protecting her lover at all costs. When the point of her athame drove into Dafoe's heart, she nearly passed out from the explosion of lethal black hatred escaping his body.

She crumpled to the ground inches from Dafoe. She heard voices. Mac's? Rick's? Regina's?

Lilith couldn't make out the sounds. Flashes of white light strobed in her brain, turning her stomach into a pit of nausea. Lies hadn't sickened her this time, but the overwhelming attack of evil had. Emotions so darkly sinister, so disgusting, Lilith couldn't wade out of them. She was only vaguely aware of someone shifting her body, embracing her. Lifting her. Loving her.

The warmth of the positive emotion curled around her even while cool air whizzed by as if she were being carried somewhere else. Only after hearing a bell—the ding of an elevator?—did her brain clear enough to see Mac's face above hers, his eyes wide with worry.

"Hey," she managed, her throat dry and her tongue thick.

His grin nearly overwhelmed her with its brilliance. "Hey, yourself."

Blinking, she fought for the strength to raise her hand and explore the shadowed skin on his chin and cheeks. "We're alive?"

"Amazing, don't you think?"

"Not half as amazing as…"

She wanted to say not half as amazing as falling in love. Not half as amazing as connecting telepathically with the man she adored. Not half as amazing as the sex they were going to have once they tried that trick in bed.

But instead Lilith snuggled against Mac's chest and drifted into unconsciousness, grinning from the erotic visions dancing through her mind.

Epilogue

STERILE ODORS OF ALCOHOL and disinfectant battled with spearmint and rosewood beneath Lilith's nose. She awoke to Josie waving a silk cloth around her face, but she didn't have the strength to swat it away.

"Where's Mac?" she asked.

Josie's grin was so bright, Lilith had to look away. "Hello to you, too."

Lilith grimaced. Her mouth was coated with sandpaper.

"Sorry. Hi. Where's Mac?"

"Outside talking to the doctor."

"How long have I been...?"

"Only a few hours. You passed out and Mac brought you here. He called me. He's been worried out of his mind. Might have hurt someone if Regina hadn't shown up. You weren't kidding about her being powerful, were you?"

Lilith managed enough strength to shake her head. Exhaustion made every molecule in her body triple in weight, and the queasiness that had overcome her earlier hadn't completely subsided. She tried to wrap her mind around all that had happened, but *fuzzy* didn't begin to describe the atmosphere in her brain. She needed answers and she didn't have the strength to reach out with her mind and get them for herself.

"What happened?"

Josie's expression darkened. She glanced around, then darted to the door, peeked out for a moment, then returned after sliding the lock in place.

She leaned close to Lilith, her voice hushed.

"The mayor is dead."

Lilith allowed her head to drift to the side. Catching sight of a foam cup, she motioned to Josie, who slid a spoonful of ice chips into her mouth.

"I know," Lilith said. "I think I killed him."

Josie's face scrunched into an unreadable mess. At least Lilith figured it was unreadable. Though she sensed she still had her psychic powers, she was simply too tired to use them.

"Regina's not sure about that."

Lilith blinked and swallowed a few more chips of ice. "What do you mean? I was there."

"Yes, but you were also connected to Mac's mind at the time, weren't you? The two of you had merged so completely, you were able to share thoughts. That's Regina's theory. She believes you acted on Mac's intentions. You destroyed a horrible person. A warlock. Regina verified all this before she sent Mac and Rick away."

"Rick?"

Josie nodded eagerly. "He showed up just after all the action had gone down. He'd been talking to me on his cell phone when you reached out to him. How cool is that? You can communicate with people psychically. I mean, how far-fetched is the theory of psychic suggestion now? You really should read the book—"

Lilith held up her hand. She loved Josie with all her heart, but the babbling didn't go over so well when her head was pounding.

"You called Regina?"

Josie nodded. "When Rick said you were calling him psychically for help, I knew you needed her. I had her number. I hope you're not angry."

Lilith wasn't sure, but patted Josie's hand softly anyway. Actually, she knew she wasn't mad at Josie. Her friend had simply acted out of worry and fear. But Lilith didn't exactly like the idea of her sister riding to her rescue. The situation rankled.

A soft knock sent Josie to the door. Seconds later, though her eyes had drifted closed, she sensed Mac on one side of her, her sister on the other.

She forced her lashes apart.

Mac was grinning like an idiot. Good goddess, she loved him. He had blood on his shirt, his skin was pale and his hands were shaking, but she still could eat him with a spoon.

"Hey," he said.

Her mind did a little dance in her head. Concentrating, she severed the connection they'd established earlier. Right now, she could deal with only one brain at a time—hers.

"Hey, yourself. Want to tell me what happened?"

Mac exchanged wary glances with Josie and Regina. After a few whispers, Josie left the room.

Regina reached down and took Lilith's hand, her long dark hair falling in a soft cascade over her shoulder. Lilith noticed that Regina had a smear of blood on her sleeve, another on her cheek.

"You vanquished some serious evil," Regina said with an impressed smile.

Lilith snorted. "You sure they didn't vanquish me in the process?"

"You overloaded your circuits by connecting to Mac, then

by the backlash of evil the warlock unleashed when he died. The Council assures me that rest and relaxation, as well as intense retraining afterward, will aid in your recovery."

Amassing all her energy, Lilith managed to shift in the bed, her muscles screaming. "You know how I feel about the Council."

"I believe you wanted them to kiss your ass," Regina said with a snicker.

She gave a quick nod. Her feelings hadn't changed. "If they hadn't waited until the very last moment to give me my powers back, I might have been able to avoid getting my butt kicked by a bad witch and an evil warlock."

"They didn't give you your powers back," Regina said.

"Excuse me? Do I have to prove I can—"

Lilith cut herself off as Regina's thoughts streamed into her brain like gentle flowing water over a thirsty riverbed. She saw images of her in Mac's car, following Boothe and Pogo into the bar. She caught a glance of her exchange with the women at the bakery and then with Josie at the shop. When a vision of her making love to Mac flashed in her mind, she connected stares with her sister.

"You've been watching me?" Lilith asked. "The whole Council? Man, gives a whole new perspective to Peeping Toms, doesn't it?"

Regina smirked. "No one watched you. I monitored the situation, yes, but what you're seeing in your mind's eye is your memory, not mine. You opened yourself up to a whole new world over the last few days. You broadened your friendship with Josie, you risked your life for someone else. You opened your heart to true honesty and love. All of the roadblocks you'd put up in your life came crashing down and you were able to not only free your powers, but grow them exponentially. You should be very proud."

"Free? You stripped them from me."

Regina glanced at her feet. "Not exactly. I just sort of hid them from you so you could find them again when you were ready."

Lilith laughed until it hurt, which only allowed a few seconds of happiness.

"Rest now."

Guilt niggled at Lilith and the experience was wholly unfamiliar. Her nose twitched as if a rotten smell had thrust up her nostrils. "I'm sorry, Regina."

"Sorry for what?" her sister asked, her lavender eyes glistening. "For not dying? For protecting me from a warlock who was amassing power by feeding a crime wave in one of the nation's largest cities?"

"That's what he was doing?" she asked, knowing she and Mac had thrown out the supposition but hadn't had time in the confrontation to clear up the details.

"Looks that way. We can't stop the drugs, but Dafoe's death will have counteracted any magical properties he'd snuck into them. I understand why you didn't call me, but never take on something this risky again, do you understand?"

Lilith arched an eyebrow at her sister's bossy tone.

Regina smiled. "When you've healed, we'll talk. I love you. Get better. The Council has great plans for you now that you've transcended your limitations."

Lilith accepted her sister's tender hug, then gave her hand a squeeze. "I love you, too. But the Council can still kiss my ass."

"I had a feeling you'd say that."

And with that, Regina shimmered out of the room.

Mac's eyes nearly bugged out of his head. "Okay, that's the

fucking weirdest thing I've ever seen, and, after tonight, that's saying a lot."

Lilith tried not to laugh at Mac's shock, but she couldn't help herself. And yet when his hand tightened around hers, the weakness threatening to overtake her dissipated and the pain dialed down a notch. She was too tired to reach out to him mentally, but the connection they'd forged during the crisis had a residual effect that made her want to crawl into his skin. Or maybe that was just lust. She wasn't sure and she didn't care, she just wanted out of this hospital and back into her bed. Or Mac's bed. She wasn't choosy.

Lilith glanced down at her hands, expecting them to be covered in blood. They were clean.

"I can't believe what I did. I'm all for breaking rules, Mac, but I've never—"

"Shh," he ordered, sweeping a kiss across her forehead as he settled into the chair beside her bed. "You did precisely what I would have done. You saved our lives."

"And Thompson?"

"Dead, too."

Lilith groaned. "And the police?"

Mac glanced aside before meeting her gaze head-on. "It would have been worse if your sister hadn't shown up. She didn't have much time, but she used a little hocus-pocus to make it look like Thompson killed Dafoe with the knife."

"But you shot Thompson," she said.

Mac's voice was a growl, as if the lies tasted nasty on his tongue. "According to your sister, forensics will prove that I shot Thompson after he stabbed the mayor. The wounds from my gun were superficial. He died of a heart attack, probably brought on by the mayor."

Lilith nodded, knowing that, in a pinch, facts could be manipulated magically in order to protect and preserve the existence of the magical world. She imagined Mac was torn to shreds over the exploitation of evidence, but what choice did they have?

"I'm sorry, Mac."

"I quit the force."

"What? No! You can't make a decision like that when your emotions are running so high. Give yourself some time to—"

He cut her off with a kiss, and after a few minutes of delicious bliss, the tension spiking through her body ebbed. When he pulled back and she glanced into his deep, dark eyes, she knew he'd done what he had to do.

"I can't be a hypocrite," he explained.

She understood. Despite the necessity of what they'd done, Mac wasn't the type of man to live easily with lies and secrets. How could he lead his cops and admonish them to be honest in their investigations when he hadn't been?

"What about Rick?"

Mac shook his head. "He's a mess. He walked in just before Regina showed up and saw the whole thing, but took off ahead of security and the uniforms who answered your 911 call. As soon as you're released, Josie's going to look for him."

Lilith tried to sit up and was surprised by the burgeoning strength in her arms. "Rick will be okay. He has a lot to process, but he's a believer in good over evil. That will be his bottom line."

Mac grinned. "Is that an educated prediction or a psychic insight?"

She did feel stronger. The pain in her body had subsided and the fog had lifted from her brain. Filling her lungs with sanitized air, she focused on his question and the answer formed slowly in her head.

"A bit of both," she replied. She had a ton of questions. How had she and Mac connected telepathically? Was it permanent? How did Mac explain her injuries to the police? Or had he? Did the cops even know she was there? She decided to leave the details for later, trusting that Regina had cleared things up as best as possible. The rest they'd deal with on their own.

For now, they had to focus on the future.

"What next?" she asked.

"The doctor signs you out and I take you home."

She yanked the wires and tubes off her body, ignoring his protesting scowl. Mundane medicine hadn't healed her wounds. She just needed time. And Mac. Lots and lots of Mac.

He grabbed her clothes from a chair and laid them beside her on the bed.

"And then?"

"Your sister says she thinks it's time to revitalize the protection squads. Apparently Thompson was once on a squad in Europe and faked his own death to escape to the city and hook up with Dafoe. If a punk like him could make the team, I figure I'm a shoo-in. I asked her for an interview," he informed her.

"But you're a mundane!" Lilith protested, the thought of Mac running up against evil magical beings on a regular basis striking pure, unadulterated terror through her body.

"I did fine tonight," he boasted.

"You had me," Lilith reminded him sharply.

He undid the ties on the back of her hospital gown. "And I plan to always have you. We'll train up. Perfect that telepathic thing we've got going. Did I ever tell you my great-grandmother on my mother's side had the Sight? We'll be hell to deal with as a pair."

The energy in Mac's voice traveled down to his fingertips. Skimming over her flesh as he helped her dress, he sparked a thousand possibilities in Lilith's mind, each more delicious and exciting and sensual than the last. They had worked very well together when they'd simply been a psychic and a cop. Last night, they'd pushed farther than she'd ever imagined, watching each other's backs, facing down powerful evil together—their minds interlocked—and making it out alive. Maybe the protection squads did need a shot of out-of-the-box thinking...and who better to provide it than a rule-breaking psychic and a mundane with courage and conviction to equal his good sense?

And besides, their telepathic connection had started when they'd made love. If constant, uninterrupted training in the bedroom was required to hone that skill, who was she to argue?

"I can't believe you've adjusted to my crazy world so easily," she said once she was out of the hospital gown and comfortable in her own clothes.

Mac enveloped her in his arms and kissed her long and hard before opening the door. Josie smiled at the two of them, then took off without another word, anxious, no doubt, to find her man and conjure up her own happy ending.

"Part of me is just operating on adrenaline," Mac said, his arms still wrapped tightly around her. "The other part doesn't care if magic exists or it doesn't so long as we're together."

Lilith melded her body to Mac's, languishing in the way his hardness struck her body like a match. A tingle traveled from the tips of her toes to the roots of her hair, a combination of the magic she was born with and the magic that came from two people who'd connected at the center of their souls. "You couldn't strip me away from you if you tried," Lilith said.

"Oh, I'm going to strip you all right," Mac said hungrily, "but not in the way you think."

"How do you know what I'm thinking?" she asked, her tone saucy.

He chuckled, buried his face in her neck and suckled the skin just beneath her earlobe until she no longer remembered the question.

Not that it mattered, because no matter what Mac asked her, from now until always, Lilith's answer would be, "Yes, yes, yes."

* * * * *

The war of the witches isn't quite over...
check out Regina's story in next month's
WITCHY BUSINESS from Harlequin Books.
For a sneak peek, turn the page...

FILLING HER LUNGS WITH the smoldering night air, Regina St. Lyon closed her eyes tightly and chanted. After one verse, she tripped over the words. She cursed, struggling to remember the phrases in the right order, to speak the forbidden language of her Wiccan ancestors with the right inflections. She took another deep breath and nearly choked on the mixed scents of charred herbs, burned grass, singed skin and blood. The blood of her beloved.

"Regina, don't do this," Brock demanded. He'd dropped to his knees, pain evident in each syllable he uttered. His face, once so devastatingly handsome, now was simply devastated.

Regina's palm still simmered from the magical burst of energy she'd used to defend herself. He'd betrayed her. And if she didn't recite the forbidden curse now to banish him to the middle realm, he'd destroy her entire race.

She squeezed her eyelids tighter, blocking out the sight of the man she'd once loved, holding back the rush of tears threatening to burst through. She hadn't asked to be chosen as Guardian of Witches, but the responsibilities had been bred into her from birth. She hadn't asked for her mother to die, forcing the Council to coronate Regina as Guardian when she was only sixteen. She certainly hadn't asked for Brock Aegis to sneak into her life fifteen years later, posing as a male witch seeking help from the Registry of Witches so he could seduce her and then to turn on her like the Hunter he was. She hadn't asked for this heartbreak, but now, as always, she had to stand strong.

She had to destroy him before he destroyed her.

She chanted again and again until the intonations spilled off her lips like the rush of a swift river. She opened her eyes, calm as she surrounded herself with the power of her ancestors. Her mother. Her grandmother. Her great-grandmother and great-great-aunt—all women of the St. Lyon line charged with the protection of the witching world, from the nonmagical mundanes who followed the tenets of Wicca to the magical sacreds who, like her, possessed powers at odds with the laws of physics and nature.

As the magic stirred, Brock tried to stand. The ground around him shook. Cracked. Still, he straightened and balanced his body, squared his shoulders and locked his eyes on her, his mouth dropping open when he realized what she had done.

She'd opened the portal to the middle realm.

"Regina," he said, his voice dropping in volume, but not in intensity. She didn't want to stare into his wide, black eyes, but she could not look away. Until he was gone, she'd forever be under his spell—trapped by the grand illusion of love and devotion that had nearly cost her her life.

"You gave me no choice, Brock. You hunted me. You caught me. But now your prey has broken free."

He opened his mouth to speak again, but the vibration of the ground around him cut him short. The crust of the Earth split in a spiderweb of cracks around him. The Hunter had become the quarry, about to be swallowed by the source of all witching power.

Brock gave her a nod. Had he accepted his fate? Around him, rocks burst into the air and columns of red-hot steam spiraled into the sky.

Regina locked her knees, bracing herself for his descent, but her legs shook so violently she had to grab on to the nearest tree. When a root shot out of the ground like a snake and slithered toward Brock, she swallowed a scream.

She wanted to stop this. She wanted to save him from a fate that rivaled death in its cruelty. But despite the tears clouding her vision, Regina knew she'd acted as Guardian in the fullest sense—sacrificing her own heart in the process. The heart he'd tricked, lied to and broken.

The dirt-encrusted roots slid across the ground from four directions. With his eyes trained on her, Brock held out his arms to the monstrous vines. They twined around him, binding his wrists, ankles, midsection and neck. He didn't protest, didn't curse, didn't speak a single word even when the roots yanked him down through the broken ground and into the tempest below.

Regina fell to the ground at the same second he disappeared. As the clearing reformed, erasing all evidence of the battle, Regina allowed herself to weep for her humiliation and for her loss. By the time she'd calmed, the clearing where she'd led Brock had returned to normal. Crickets and frogs sang in the distance. Wind rustled softly through the verdant leaves.

Except for the sound of her ragged breathing, no one who stumbled into this park on the grounds of the Registry would ever know the violence that had erupted here—all at her hand.

"Regina."

She shot to her feet, her muscles protesting, searching for the source of the sound.

"Regina."

"Brock?" she responded.

She glanced at the ground at the center of the clearing where she'd formed the ancient circle and banished her lover to the underworld. Not even a blade of grass looked out of place.

"Regina, wake up."

His voice sounded hollow, as if far away. Stumbling, she made her way to the core of the clearing and pawed at the ground. It was solid. He was trapped. She'd used the forbidden curse. No magic, not even the powerful spells handed down from her ancestors, could undo his doom.

"Regina, please. You have to remember. There isn't much time."

Suddenly a choking sensation gripped her. She clawed at her throat, trying to relieve the invisible pressure strangling the breath out of her. Her hands made contact with the platinum chain she wore around her neck, and the metal burned.

And then broke away.

She gasped for air. Her eyes snapped open, jolting her out of her nightmare and into the cold reality of her room. The full moon just outside her uncovered window threw ice-blue streaks across her bed. She was drenched with sweat, her sheets coiled around her body, tangling with the silk boxers and T-shirt she'd worn to sleep. Beside her, incense smoldered, injecting the air with the lingering perfume of lavender and sandalwood, meant to calm her. The herbs had failed miserably. Her heart was still trying to pound its way through her ribs. Her lungs, fed by ragged breaths, ached inside her chest.

She dragged her hand to her neck and this time registered the absence of her talisman.

"Looking for this?"

He emerged from the shadows boots first, the leather dirty and torn. His jeans, ripped at the seams, hung loosely, as if his muscles had atrophied or body weight had simply melted off his normally powerful frame. His shirt still held the stains of his injuries from their battle. Dried blood mingled with the smoky streaks of scorch marks.

She remembered.

All of it. Every detail. Every emotion.

With a thought, she sparked the lamp beside her bed. The glow instantly reflected off the amulet he dangled between his grimy fingers. The alexandrite, nearly the size of her palm, shined purplish-red in the incandescent light. Brock had not only returned from the middle realm where she'd banished him three months ago, he'd stolen the talisman she'd enchanted to block the memories of him from her mind—memories wrenched from the darkest recesses of her soul. Memories that kept her from performing as Guardian.

"Give it back," she demanded.

"So you can forget about me again? Forget what you did to me?"

"I had no choice." She wrestled to remove the tangled sheets from her body. When she succeeded, she slid off the bed and faced him. She jutted her chin forward even as her betrayed heart screamed for her to crumble into a mottled mess on the floor. "You came to Sedona to kill me. Or did you expect I'd let you murder me simply because you'd tricked your way into my bed?"

He dropped his hand, the talisman dangling at his side. The

spell she'd cast over the ancient stone of her ancestors would no longer keep the memories at bay. She had no idea how, but Brock had returned. Now she would need her painful memories to protect the Registry. To protect her people. To protect her heart.

"No. I mean, yes, I intended to destroy you," he explained, his voice raspy. "But I never meant to…I never meant to love you."

"Spare me, Brock! How can I accept the word of a Hunter? You were born and raised with one motive, just as I was. But while I was trained to protect my people, you were trained to destroy us. I cannot change who I am any more than you."

"I have changed."

Regina's bitter laugh rent the suddenly stifling aromatic air. "You are a Hunter. How many witches did you kill before you found me, Brock? How many?"

He took a step forward, but Regina stopped him by raising her palm. As the Guardian, she possessed a rare and terrible power—the ability to harness energy and concentrate it into a ball of electric pain that she could hurl at will. The energy bursts had given her the upper hand in her battle with Brock three months ago. Why did she hesitate now?

"Regina, there isn't time for me to explain, but I've come back to save you."

"Save me from what? I survived *you*. What could possibly be worse?"

Brock threw Regina's talisman on the bed, his shoulders taut and his eyes dark. A shiver rippled from the hairs on the surface of her skin to deep inside her belly.

"Old Movert," he replied.

Regina's chest tightened under the weight of this enemy's name.

"Old Movert is a myth. He doesn't exist."

Brock chuckled, but his laugh contained not a hint of mirth or happiness. "You're wrong. Old Movert is very, very real. You'll know that for yourself soon, when he comes here to kill you."

* * * * *

Welcome to cowboy country...

Turn the page for a sneak preview of
TEXAS BABY
by
Kathleen O'Brien
An exciting new title from
Harlequin Superromance
for everyone who loves stories about the West.

Harlequin Superromance—
Where life and love weave together in
emotional and unforgettable ways.

CHAPTER ONE

CHASE TRANSFERRED his gaze to the road and identified a foreign spot on the horizon. A car. Almost half a mile away, where the straight, tree-lined drive met the public road. He could tell it was coming too fast, but judging the speed of a vehicle moving straight toward you was tricky.

It wasn't until it was about two hundred yards away that he realized the driver must be drunk...or crazy. Or both.

The guy was going maybe sixty. On a private drive, out here in ranch country, where kids or horses or tractors or stupid chickens might come darting out any minute, that was criminal. Chase straightened from his comfortable slouch and waved his hands.

"Slow down, you fool," he called out. He took the porch steps quickly and began walking fast down the driveway.

The car veered oddly, from one lane to another, then up onto the slight rise of the thick green spring grass. It just barely missed the fence.

"Slow down, damn it!"

He couldn't see the driver, and he didn't recognize this automobile. It was small and old, and couldn't have cost much even when it was new. It was probably white, but now it needed either a wash or a new paint job or both.

"Damn it, what's wrong with you?"

At the last minute, he had to jump away, because the idiot behind the wheel clearly wasn't going to turn to avoid a collision. He couldn't believe it. The car kept coming, finally slowing a little, but it was too late.

Still going about thirty miles an hour, it slammed into the large, white-brick pillar that marked the front boundaries of the house. The pillar wasn't going to give an inch, so the car had to. The front end folded up like a paper fan.

It seemed to take forever for the car to settle, as if the trauma happened in slow motion, reverberating from the front to the back of the car in ripples of destruction. The front windshield suddenly seemed to ice over with lethal bits of glassy frost. Then the side windows exploded.

The front driver's door wrenched open, as if the car wanted to expel its contents. Metal buckled hideously. Small pieces, like hubcaps and mirrors, skipped and ricocheted insanely across the oyster-shell driveway.

Finally, everything was still. Into the silence, a plume of steam shot up like a geyser, smelling of rust and heat. Its snake-like hiss almost smothered the low, agonized moan of the driver.

Chase's anger had disappeared. He didn't feel anything but a dull sense of disbelief. Things like this didn't happen in real life. Not in his life. Maybe the sun had actually put him to sleep….

But he was already kneeling beside the car. The driver was a woman. The frosty glass-ice of the windshield was dotted with small flecks of blood. She must have hit it with her head, because just below her hairline a red liquid was seeping out. He touched it. He tried to wipe it away before it reached her eyebrow, though, of course that made no sense at all. Her eyes were shut.

Was she conscious? Did he dare move her? Her dress was covered in glass, and the metal of the car was sticking out lethally in all the wrong places.

Then he remembered, with an intense relief, that every good medical man in the county was here, just behind the house, drinking his champagne. He found his phone and paged Trent.

The woman moaned again.

Alive, then. Thank God for that.

He saw Trent coming toward him, starting out at a lope, but quickly switching to a full run.

"Get Dr. Marchant," Chase called. "Don't bother with 911."

Trent didn't take long to assess the situation. A fraction of a second, and he began pulling out his cell phone and running toward the house.

The yelling seemed to have roused the woman. She opened her eyes. They were blue and clouded with pain and confusion.

"Chase," she said.

His breath stalled. His head pulled back. "What?"

Her only answer was another moan, and he wondered if he had imagined the word. He reached around her and put his arm behind her shoulders. She was tiny. Probably petite by nature, but surely way too thin. He could feel her shoulder blades pushing against her skin, as fragile as the wishbone in a turkey.

She seemed to have passed out, so he put his other arm under her knees and lifted her out. He tried to avoid the jagged metal, but her skirt caught on a piece and the tearing sound seemed to wake her again.

"No," she said. "Please."

"I'm just trying to help," he said. "It's going to be all right."

She seemed profoundly distressed. She wriggled in his

arms, and she was so weak, like a broken bird. It made him feel too big and brutish. And intrusive. As if touching her this way, his bare hands against the warm skin behind her knees, were somehow a transgression.

He wished he could be more delicate. But he smelled gasoline, and he knew it wasn't safe to leave her here.

Finally he heard the sound of voices, as guests began to run around the side of the house, alerted by Trent. Dr. Marchant was at the front, racing toward them as if he were forty instead of seventy. Susannah was right behind him, her green dress floating around her trim legs.

"Please," the woman in his arms murmured again. She looked at him, the expression in her blue eyes lost and bewildered. He wondered if she might be on drugs. Hitting her head on the windshield might account for this unfocused, glazed look, but it couldn't explain the crazy driving.

"Please, put me down. Susannah… The wedding…"

Chase's arms tightened instinctively, and he froze in his tracks. She whimpered, and he realized he might be hurting her. "Say that again?"

"The wedding. I have to stop it."

* * * * *

Be sure to look for TEXAS BABY,
*available September 11, 2007,
as well as other fantastic Superromance titles
available in September.*

REQUEST YOUR FREE BOOKS!

2 FREE NOVELS PLUS 2 FREE GIFTS!

HARLEQUIN®
Blaze

Red-hot reads!

H807

ATHENA FORCE

Heart-pounding romance and thrilling adventure.

Professional negotiator Lindsey Novak
is faced with her biggest challenge—to
buy back Teal Arnett, a young woman with
unique powers. In the process Lindsey
uncovers a devastating plot that involves
scientists from around the globe, and all of
them lead to one woman who is bent on
destroying Athena Academy...at any cost.

LOOK FOR

THE GOOD THIEF

by Judith Leon

*Available September
wherever you buy books.*

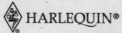

HARLEQUIN®

Blaze™

COMING NEXT MONTH

#345 KIDNAPPED! Jo Leigh
Forbidden Fantasies
She had a secret desire to be kidnapped and held against her will.... But when heiress Tate Baxter's fantasy game turns out to be all too real, can sexy bodyguard Michael Caulfield put aside his feelings and rescue her in time?

#346 MY SECRET LIFE Lori Wilde
The Martini Dares, Bk. 1
Kate Winfield's secrets were safe until hottie Liam James came along. Now the sexy bachelor with the broad chest and winning smile is insisting he wants to uncover the delectable Katie—from head to toe.

#347 OVEREXPOSED Leslie Kelly
The Bad Girls Club, Bk. 3
Isabella Natale works in the family bakery by day, but at night her velvet mask and G-string drive men wild. Her double life is a secret, even from Nick Santori, the club's hot new bodyguard who's always treated her like a kid. Now she's planning to show the man of her dreams that while it's okay to look, it's *much* better to touch....

#348 SWEPT AWAY Dawn Atkins
Sex on the Beach
Her plan was simple. Candy Calder would use her vacation to show her boss Matt Rockwell she was serious about her job. But her plan backfired when he invited her to enjoy the sinful side of Malibu. With an offer this tempting, what girl could refuse?

#349 SHIVER AND SPICE Kelley St. John
The Sexth Sense, Bk. 3
She's not alive. She's not dead. She's something in between. And medium Dax Vicknair wants her desperately! Dax fell madly in love with teacher Celeste Beauchamp when he helped one of her students cross over. He thought he was destined to live without her. But now Celeste is back—and Dax intends to make the most of their borrowed time....

#350 THE NAKED TRUTH Shannon Hollis
Million Dollar Secrets, Bk. 3
Risk taker Eve Best is on the verge of having everything she's ever wanted. But what she really wants is the handsome buttoned-down executive Mitchell Hayes, who must convince the gorgeous talk-show host to say "yes" to his business offer *and* his very private proposition....